**"You're so lucky having your best friend live so close to you. Mine lives on another planet."** Oh, stars, what did I just say? Why is it as a humanoid I can't control my mouth?

"You're right, Nic, she is really funny and cute, too," Josh said.

He looked sideways at me, and I got really warm. Maybe that's what she meant when she said Josh had the hots for me. He did make me warm. Funny how I could feel hot, though, when my skin looked like a chicken's, all covered in small bumps.

He stopped in the middle of the cement and turned me around to face him. He reached forward and touched my nose. So I did what any ananoid would do, I slapped him. Not nearly as effective as when I used my antenna, but it had the same result.

Oops, I don't think I was supposed to do that. I might have put his nose out of joint.

"What the snap was that for? I was just wiping a bit of ice cream off your nose. Man, you pack a wallop." He bent over with his head in his hands, and his ball cap fell to the ground.

I bent down to pick it up, figuring it was the least I could do, and realized I'd made another mistake...

# I Was a Teenage Alien

by

## Jane Greenhill

I Was a Teenage Alien

Cover Art by *Kim Mendoza*

The Wild Rose Press
PO Box 708
Adams Basin, NY 14410-0706
Visit us at www.thewildrosepress.com

Publishing History
First Climbing Rose Edition, 2008
Print ISBN 1-60154-443-X


Published in the United States of America

## Praise for I Was a Teenage Alien

"Jane Greenhill's book, *I Was a Teenage Alien*, gives you a wild galactic ride into laughter you won't want to end."

~Teresa Reasor, author of
*Willy C. Sparks, The Dragon Who Lost His Fire*

## Dedication

To my boys who look to the stars and see the
possibilities

Chapter One

"Your brother is being a pain and won't answer his nose piece," my handler Zen whined, his hands flittering around like he was swatting the lower echelons of our race.

I pulled a *wad* of *gysogtom* out of my ear, turning off the music. Why is it someone always wants to talk to you just as your favorite song comes on? Major annoying, but then anything to do with my brother rubbed my antennas the wrong way. No matter where he was, he managed to ruin my fun. I slipped the *wad* into its protective foil sheet and tucked it into my cheek for safekeeping. I have a horrible habit of putting my *wad* down somewhere and forgetting where I left it.

Stars above, my mother was always on my back. She'd ream me out in the high-pitched, nauseating voice she kept for just that occasion. "*Wad*s don't grow on trees."

Actually, they did, but try and tell my mother anything she didn't want to hear, and you might as well talk to Pluto, because if she didn't want to listen, she'd tune you out. How completely typical of an adult. You wouldn't see a teen ananoid being so careless regarding another's feelings. Well, okay, actually you would, but we do it with a little more finesse.

Zen fumed, his antennas twitching a mile a minute. I had to look away. I got dizzy trying to keep track of them.

"Zen, tell me something I don't know! He's always a pain. That's what you get for sending him to Earth. I begged to go but, nope, Earth was no

1

place for a girl from Zorca-twenty-three. So suffer!" I folded my wings and sat back on my triads.

Great! Wonderful! Perfect! Here I was stuck on Zorca-twenty-three, a planet three stars away from the yucky Space Station the Earthlings are building because they ruined their own planet. Now they want to start wrecking something they can destroy for infinity. But don't get me started there. I might be a teenage ananoid, but my opinion still matters, at least to me.

"Well, it looks like you're going to get your wish. In my hot little triad are orders for you to bring Ralb home," Zen said, viewing a hologram that appeared on the cave wall in front of us.

"Too bad! I'm not going." I reached into my cheek and searched for my *wad*. I had better things to do than hunt all over the polluted planet for my dweeb of a brother. Besides I had a date tonight and had to get ready. It took a long time to wash and fluff one's antennas.

Some things, okay, most everything, was more important than my brother, at least to me. He was three birthings younger than me, but he was the eldest male in our family, so he got all the privileges. It bugged me to no end. Just because his eyes were situated in a different position than mine, he got the highest rock in the cave to call his own. Life on planet Zorca-twenty-three was just not fair.

"What is it with you teenage ananoids? One eon you're begging to do something. Then as soon as you're allowed to do it, you don't want to!" His lower eye quivered in frustration.

One way to tell the male and the female species of our race apart is the location of our three eyes. Mewls have theirs in a row one on top of the other, which I personally think is hideous. I, for example, have mine in a row side by side, which is much more attractive and appealing. We are—not to brag—

highly evolved, praying mantis. When mewls get upset, their top eye flops around, again most unattractive.

I had to listen to Zen's complaining about, well, my complaining. I was glad I'd closed my verbal diary. I so didn't want to hear his nagging when I opened the pages again.

"Did I ask for this life?" Zen picked up a comb and ran it through his antennas, trying to untangle them. "No way! Stupid me. I thought: How hard can it be to keep a couple of teenage ananoids in line? Cricket. If you're not breaking your curfew by staying out late with that no good Fronzy, then you're not picking up after yourself."

"Fronzy was so last week. I'm not seeing him anymore," I said, embarrassed he was aware of my social life. Or in my case, lack of one. I shook my eyes, ridding myself of the memory of my former Best Ananoid Friend who shall remain nameless swapping antenna spit with Fronzy. Not only did I lose my supposed boyfriend, but even more importantly I lost my BAF, Kaj. Oops, I wasn't going to say her name. Oh, well, she's not important anyway, since she's no longer with us.

But just as I prepared to toss my heart over the top of Mount Annable, I saw Gorget. He was visiting from the other side of Zorca-twenty-three and was ten eons better looking than Fronzy. Gorget had a droopy middle eye that made my antennas twitter.

The best part, though, was he met my former BAF before her demise and told me I was a million times better looking. A typical humanoid concern (what someone of the mawl species thought of me), but some things are universally cosmic.

Zen droned on and on as if he didn't hear me. "I should have listened to my handler and become a black-hole hairdresser. Never run out of work, and the ananoids are so unused to hair it doesn't matter what it looks like, they're happy. Happy, I say."

"It's not too late," I said, wondering what I'd look like with hair. If I had my choice, I'd have it cut and styled like the Parental Being on the television show, *Married with Children*. Every week I tuned in to watch the show on the satellite. Peg Bundy was my hero. I loved her hairstyle, and the way she dressed was to die for. Not to really die, of course, but I'm sure you catch my continental drift.

He leaned toward me, his top eye blowing in the breeze. "Missy, you're going. And that's the last I want to hear on the subject."

I wondered if I'd be able to find a neon mini-skirt like Peg wore on the last episode. I tried to cross my antennas so no one was aware. I could only hope.

Zen could be as stubborn as me, and he'd had a heck of a lot more practice.

"Whatever!" I said, as I tried to control my twittering antenna. I didn't want Zen to see I was thrilled to be going. I'd just have to put Gorget on hold until I came back, if I did. Wow, talk about playing hard to get. "Do I get any training? Any resources?"

"According to the letter"—He waved the white mist in front of my three eyelids—"you are to head over to Assessment and get the T-gene." He turned away from me and muttered, "Though with your parental history, I'm sure you're not going to need it."

I was about to ask him what the heck he was talking about—my femawl Parental Being never ventured further than the ananoid center where she babysat, and my mawl Parental Being was too busy working trying to keep food in all his offspring—but then I realized where he was sending me.

"Zen, I hate it when they poke and probe my body. Can't I just go without it? I'm sure I'll manage fine." My voice sounded smug to my own antennas. "I completed the mission when I was sent to that stupid Space Station. Why did they build that monstrosity so close to our planet? The light shines in my eyes, no matter what time of day or night. Remember how I snuck over and borrowed their food? We were able to reproduce it. Yep, thanks to me, we are now the planet known for having M burgers in yellow wrappers."

"Yes, and we are all eternally grateful for your spy mission. Never mind that you were sent to find out how their electrons worked, but I guess to a teen it's more important to fill one's stomach than one's brain with knowledge."

"If you took the time to watch television, you'd realize there are more M burgers in yellow wrappers than there are Space Stations. That should tell you the importance humanoids put on their meat products."

Zen sighed. It was so loud Gorget's family on the other side of the planet could hear it. "You're about to become one of them, Oas, so you'd be wise to keep your opinions to yourself."

"Fine, whatever!" I said, wondering if I would be older or younger when I got to Planet Earth.

He wet his mandible and flipped through a stationary manual. "Right. You're to be reminded you can only stay a maximum of six months."

"Why? Does my visa expire?" I asked sarcastically. Everyone who's anyone knows those magic little cards are good for at least five years.

"No, Zorcans in human form can only survive for a short period of time, whereas humanoids can survive on our planet for eons."

"Yeah, sure." I let out a breath of air I hadn't realized I'd been holding. "Like anyone who had the opportunity to live on Earth would ever leave that glorious colorful planet for this pile of rocks.

Jane Greenhill

"You'd be surprised." Zen reached into the sub-zero container and, using all of his triads, lifted out a mist book about the size of an M burger in yellow wrapper. Fog hovered around it, slowly dispersing as the warm air in the cave came in contact with it.

Finally, the vapor dried, I was pleased to see my name etched on the cover of the book. Wow, I was officially a worldwide space traveler. This was more official than an interplanetary passport. Only problem was I wasn't going to fill it up with really cool stamps like the humanoids do when they travel to different countries.

A glow emanated from inside the book as he opened it and flipped through the pages.

I was about to ask Zen about the contents when he interrupted my thought process. "Oh, according to page three of the mist book, your new name is April. Ralb's name on planet Earth is Bertie Star."

"What kind of a name is April, Zen? Can't I keep my original one?" I begged. It's kind of cool, even if it does stand for Older Annoying Sister, at least according to Ralb. I didn't want an alias, or an AKA. I wanted to keep my old name. Maybe this planet traveling wasn't going to be so hot after all.

"Oas, don't start," he said, handing me the book. "This is why I didn't want you to go in the first place. You're never happy."

"That is so not true. Can you blame me for wanting to keep my own name? Would you like to go to Earth and be called Ben instead of Zen?" I asked, folding my triads.

"Ben is a very respected name on the planet Earth. Why, there's Ben Franklin who was a famous American president."

"There's also Benedict Arnold who wasn't so popular, and besides Ben Franklin wasn't a president. He was an inventor," I said. Realizing the conversation wasn't going to win me any friends, I

6

dropped it.

"April is the name of the month, which is how Earthlings mark the passing of the seasons. But for us it's a code name: A.P.R.I.L.—Alien Person Representing Intelligent Life."

"Zen, why don't they just count on their antenna like we do? Naming the months sounds barbaric." I held the book like it was a first class ticket to the fastest asteroid. I'd need this smoggy passport to survive in the weird culture of Earth. Old television shows were only going to take me so far.

"Obviously, they aren't as intelligent as we are. That's why we had to populate their planet," he boasted.

"Yes, I know. I remember my grandmother telling me the story of how she sent Uncle Forzon on the asteroid to settle the latest planet discovered in our solar system. What a terrible time it was for families, knowing they might never see their sons or daughters again!"

Reality hit me like a meteorite shower. "Why am I traveling thirty-nine light years again? Ralb will be fine on his own. He got himself into this mess. He can just get himself out. Only downside I can think of is we might never see him again, and then I'd be an only child, just me and my six hundred and ninety-eight siblings."

"Ralb will not be fine on his own. How can you be an only child with six hundred and ninety-eight siblings? Never mind." His left antenna rotated in a circular motion. "He should never have gone in the first place. If he hadn't decided to run away from home and sneak onto the passing asteroid by hiding in the rock crevice, he never would have been sent. His number was quite high up in the draft. By the time they called it, the quest to fill the asteroid would have been completed."

I was disgusted and, when I got upset my eye

wobbled, my left one. I drew myself up to my full height of six decimeters and puffed out my pedicel. I was a force to be reckoned with. No wonder the femawls ran my planet. "Did you have anything to do with him having a high number?

He ignored my eyes. All of his looked the other way. My antenna whipped around like a cowboy's lasso, which I had seen on one of the old black and white television shows. "You did, didn't you? Did my Parental Being put you up to that? Did she bribe you? Promise to make you the happiest ananoid on our planet?"

He shrugged his triad. "Maybe, maybe not."

"You are supposed to be my handler, and you're such a child," I said with arrogance. "I know she had her hand in here somewhere. Ralb always was her favorite."

My Parental Being flew into the room, landing precisely between Zen and me. She must have antennas built into the back of her flat, scaly head because she always barged in at the most inopportune time. This was a perfect example.

"Don't start that again! I love all my little ananoids the same."

"Yeah, right!" I was so angry, even my antennas were folded. "You mean to tell me you love all seven hundred of us the same. I find it hard to believe you don't have even a slight favoritism." I flittered my three eyelids in disbelief. "I bet you don't even know what my favorite movie is?"

"Zen, are you still allowing them to pick up the satellite signals on their third eye? I thought we had a discussion about that." My Parental Being puffed her stomach.

I was glad I wasn't the one on the receiving end of *the look.*

"They are only to watch television through the mainframe so we can control what they watch. You know there's only trash on that signal. I'd like them to be outside playing, not inside watching the space junk."

Hey, where do you think I learned my attitude? Though my mother had one up on me. She had an extra eye, one in the back of her head. Once you gave birth to ananoids, you grew one. All I can say is, thank stars, she didn't grow one for every ananoid she had. Can you imagine having a mother with seven hundred eyes? You'd never be able to get away with anything.

"See, she didn't answer my question. She doesn't know what my favorite anything is." I held up an antenna that had been dragging on the bottom of the pit. "Mother, don't try and defend yourself to me. I know where I stand with you, and it's okay. Really! I've come to the realization that because I don't have a wizzywilly, I'm not as important as the male of the species."

"Zen, who puts these crazy ideas into her head?" She shook her head. "What am I going to do with her?"

"I won't be a concern anymore. I'm off to the Planet Earth to bring back your favorite son." I ignored her as I flipped through the mist book, not really seeing any of the pages. But it gave me something to do with my triads and somewhere to look.

"When you're a mother, you'll see what I mean!" She continued her rant, "It's impossible to love one more than the other. Just impossible." Turning to Zen, she continued, "Is she going to be safe? Will she have everything she needs to get herself and Ralb home safely?"

"Don't you worry. They'll be fine. Ralb is a smart boy. He'll make sure they get back."

"Ralb is clever? What about me? Huh. If I'd gone in the first place, we wouldn't need to send a reconnaissance mission to get me home." I snapped the mist book shut, causing a cloud of vapors to engulf me. I sneezed and coughed, but quickly regained myself. I didn't want to look like a wimp. If I couldn't handle a couple of cloudy pages, they'd think I wouldn't be able to handle traveling to the other end of our solar system by myself.

"True," my mother admitted. "But neither one of you was supposed to go."

"Is that why you bribed Zen to give Ralb a high draft number?" I asked, picking at my antenna, like I didn't really care what her answer would be.

"I love you all the same, and I don't want anything to happen to any of you." She flew closer, her attention focused on me. Finally. I'd waited for this moment my whole life. This was the time I'd dreamt about. When I finally had my Parental Being's attention all to myself. I held my breath and waited for words of wisdom and her undying love to caress my antennas.

"Take a coat. If you end up in Canada, I've heard it's chilly."

Chapter Two

Good thing Zen was a whiz at math, because if they'd left the flight times for me to figure out, I would have ended up on Mars. Then my Parental Being would have been really ticked off.

I left her before I said something I'd regret for the rest of my days. That's the thing about ananoids; we live quite a long time, which has its good and bad side, mostly bad.

I flew over to the Assessment Pod. I glanced at our three moons to orient myself. I'm lousy with directions and could get lost on a one-way airoport strip. Our planet has three moons orbiting it that we see day or night. Zorca-twenty-three is in the constellation Aries, which in my opinion makes us the bossiest of the constellations. My real BFF, Lehcarr lives in the constellation Libra, and she's really easygoing. Well, as much as a Venus Fly Trap can be. She would never try to steal my boyfriend. Maybe eat him, but sometimes that hunger was beyond her control.

On our little rock we call home, I had to make my way into the Pod. It was a large mushroom-shaped boulder with a combination on its door. Believe me, having a lock was a necessity. It changed with the circling of the moons. It separated the wheat from the shaft and kept out the riff-raff, as they like to say on Earth. You think Earth has problems. You should try to keep peace between insects and plants. The plants always feel like they're undervalued, while the insects insist they are doing all the work keeping the planet up and running. Then if you had Venus Fly Traps eating the insects, and insects stealing from plants, things got downright mean and dirty. Pretty ugly. We tried to find a way to co-exist, but it wasn't always easy. One good thing, though, was that Venus Fly traps only came to visit and, thankfully, didn't stay very long.

Once I keyed in the combo written in my mist book, I crawled through a crevice to get my necessary genes for travel, glad I hadn't had that extra M burger last night or I might have gotten stuck. It was a major rite of passage I was allowed inside. Only unique ananoids of a certain age knew it was here.

I felt special, but I was here on business, an Earth-seeking ananoid.

I folded my wings and strutted into the tiny slice between the two rock faces. Each of my three eyes took in a different area of the Pod. My left eye checked all the tubes and tables lined up against the side of the cave. My right saw the counters that were used to experiment on different species. On a table floating at my top eye level was an Edorick.

The Edoricks are so stupid. They are the dodo birds of our solar system. They're as easy to catch as mosquitoes. Yes, we have those pesky insects too but, anyway, to get back to the Edoricks, they are the "famous"—and I'm making antenna quotes here—aliens you see in pictures. They have big eyes and heads that look like question marks. They are more anorexic than any supermodel I've seen on Earth. And they are so stupid.

Not only did they make themselves known to the humanoids by crashing into a place called Area Fifty-one, but they also had to pay the United States government money to cover up the fact that they were real. The government was apparently afraid humanoids would panic if they found out there's life on other planets. Get real! If humans were scared of

Edoricks, then they had some major problems besides global warming and the melting of the polar ice cap.

We on Zorca-twenty-three have a favorite joke: How many Edoricks does it take to screw in a *nftsbolb*? None, because they are just so darn stupid. I know, I know, it's a horrible joke, but we're known for our intelligence in the solar system, not our wit.

"Xron, hello," I called out as I entered the walkway leading to his lab. One thing you didn't want to do was sneak up on Xron. Take it from someone who knows. I did it once, and I'm lucky I'm around to tell the tale of what happened.

I had been sent by Zen to the Assessment Pod to get a G-gene. Zen was going to take it and add it to his soda. I learned more than just how to make hamburgers in shiny yellow paper when I went to the Space Station. I also learned the secret recipe for cola. Let me just say, I'm very popular with the younger ananoids on my planet now. Not so much with the parents. The bubbles make our antennas burp. Not a pretty sight to have six hundred and ninety-nine ananoids making smells and rude noises all at once. And that's just my immediate family.

Anyway, I digress. Xron had been doing an investigation on a humanoid. I walked in on him and didn't identify who I was. I flew up behind him, and it was all I could do to keep my antenna from throwing up. The stuff inside humans isn't pretty. I know it all serves a function and helps them live and breathe with global warming and pollution, but, yuck, it was gross.

I should have been prepared, because on the satellite *wad* I'd seen an episode of *CSI* where they seemed to think people killing people made good entertainment. But when you see it in real time and, even worse, smell it in real time, ugh. Even now I'm about to hurl my hamburger.

Xron hovered over one of his lab tables filled with smoking test tubes. I was scared of them the first time I saw them until he told me it was his lunch. His humongous bug eyes peered out from behind round pieces of glass held in place by duct tape. He kept pushing them up closer to his eyeballs, but they kept slipping downward. Duct tape doesn't stick too well on scales.

His hair was white and stuck up in many different directions I think it pointed to every compass point. He was frazzled. Seeing Xron stressed was not a pretty sight.

There were bodies piled on top of bodies, and he had to get to them before their loved ones knew they were missing, a lot of work for one ananoid, even if it was Xron.

Yes, those alien abductions are true. But Xron isn't mean or cruel. He checks out the body cavities of humanoids and Edoricks to learn how to prolong their lives and ours. After all he's a scientist, and it's all done in the name of research. No one feels anything.

When I questioned him once about it, he said that humanoids had a high tolerance for pain. They enjoyed going to a place to have their mouthpieces drilled. So I took it to mean they actually enjoyed having their bodies checked over. No worse than going to an Earth dentist.

Now if the Edoricks had abducted you, then you were in trouble, and that was an entirely different story. As I already said, they were totally clueless when it came to anything. They thought to explore a humanoid body you had to poke and probe. They did it for fun. Not for research. The Edoricks were a sadistic species.

I chatted with one last eon. Purely by coincidence, I met him in the airport. Normally I don't talk to strange aliens, but I was bored. He had been traveling from his planet to Goptruy-sixty-seven to go to a Fry Out concert.

"So was the concert any good?" I asked, noticing his Fry Out halo swarming around his bug eyes.

"The Fry Out was far out, but I should have stayed home and listened on my *wad*. We had to hover above the stage. By stars, it was the worst concert I'd ever been to," he moaned in a voice so whiney it set my *manabids* on edge.

"Why? I thought they were a good elastic band. A little tight at places and then they stretched as far as they could go," I said, not really sure why I was continuing the conversation when all I wanted him to do was stop talking.

"That's true. But it was the worst." He nodded his oddly shaped head.

I knew I was going to regret it, but I had to ask why.

"I had to float above the stage with my friend, and we couldn't see anything. There was a big support beam in our way, and while we could hear the elastic band, we couldn't see them."

See the mentality I'm dealing with here. "So why didn't you move?"

I still remember the stunned expression on his flat, cone-shaped face to this day. It was if a *nftsbolb* went on. His eyes looked like they were about to pop out of his head, even more than normal.

"That's a good idea. I wish I had of thought of it." His bony arm reached up and slapped his even bonier hand along his forehead. I felt like doing the same thing myself.

See what I mean. Another time I got into a discussion with one about gravity. He couldn't grasp the concept he wouldn't fall off his planet.

Their doctors were our rejects, which probably explains the rotten jobs they do on autopsies. If you weren't good enough for Zorca-twenty-three, you were shipped to Edor and transformed into one of them with their big saucer-shaped eyes. One of Ralb's friends was destined for such a fate. He jumped off our planet onto a passing asteroid rather than face life on Edor.

I screwed my *wad* back into my ear and tuned into another channel. You're probably wondering how I know so much about Earth when I've never traveled there before. Well, I'll tell you. Satellite. Yep, we can hook into Earth's satellite service for free. Not as good as it sounds, though, because all we get are sitcom reruns. That's why I can't wait to get to see something else on the television screen attached to my third eye. With a *wad* in my ear and the screen over my third eye, I had a portable television system.

My Parental Being tried to monitor what we watched through the mainframe television, but Ralb (when he was here) and I had our own system for watching sitcoms, and it worked pretty well. I guess it was slightly illegal, a tad pirated, but since we didn't pay for it either way, we didn't figure we were doing anyone or anything any harm.

My third eye started twitching. Not a good sign. I was still holding my breath when I walked into the mad scientist's laboratory. Really, he was. Not mad crazy, not mad nuts, but fuming mad.

For a grown-up ananoid, there was definitely something stuck in his claw, in fact all seven of them.

"What do you want?" he asked, scurrying across the floor, his antenna dragging, a sure sign he was ticked about something or at someone. I just hoped he wasn't upset with me. You have no idea what it's like when you make an adult ananoid angry. Believe me, it's not a pretty sight, even worse than the goop that's inside the humans.

"Zen showed me the mist papers that say I'm

supposed to hop on the asteroid and head to Earth."
Even to me it sounded super unreal.

"So I'll give you a *quartem*, and you can ESP
someone who cares. I'm busy. What do you need?"
His antennas skittered—one to the left, the other at
a weird angle that defined our non-gravity system. "I
have more bodies to dissect than I have tools to tear
them apart with. See that Edorick up there. He's
being a real pain. For a stupid race, they have put in
some kind of barrier that makes it hard for me to get
through their thick skin. I'm really getting ticked off.
It's killing my anapart to cut it. And for what, I ask
you? To discover their brains are the size of a gnats.
Now what is it again you need?" He strutted off in a
different direction.

"Isn't that what you're supposed to tell me?" I
wasn't totally clueless in the ways of the world or at
least Zorca-twenty-three. Adult ananoids are so
exasperating. They seem to think the solar system
revolves around them. Yeah, right! Everyone knows
it revolves around us major beings—teen ananoids.

"Here, take one of these and two of these or
maybe it's the other way around. I don't know. It
won't kill you either way." His antenna reached over
and lifted two flasks off the shelf and dropped the
pills on top of my mist book.

The tiny round circles glowed and glimmered in
the foggy clouds, the colors swirling and dancing. He
couldn't have cared less about the rainbow of
excitement happening on my book cover. Instead, he
scurried over to the hovering counter. With a planet
moving as fast as ours, you had to make concessions.
It wasn't uncommon for tables to hang suspended,
but the supremest pain in our butkus was the fact
we didn't have gravity and, believe you me, it sucked
big time. Thank goodness, we had suction cups on
our lower anaparts to hold us down.

"What are they going to do to me? I don't like

feeling drowsy. It'll upset my *trigoze*." I felt like I was traveling at warp speed through a time tunnel, and I hadn't even boarded the vessel yet.

"Is that all you ever do—complain? No wonder you're not your mother's favorite." He quivered over to the table and selected a long slender instrument. A rock-hard lump formed in my esophagut. There was no way on Zorca-twenty-three I was going to let him get near me with that contraption.

"W-what are you planning on doing with that?" I asked as the rock in my throat grew to gigantic proportions. I felt like a frog, one of those croakers. Maybe that's where they got their name—they felt like they were croaking, trying to pass the lump in their throat.

"I use it to scratch the dried-up scales on my back that my antenna can't reach," he said as he proceeded to use it.

"Right, I knew that."

"Now, these pills are so Ralb recognizes you." He flickered his antennas and as the ends lit up, he sighed.

As he reached for another vial, the lid spun off the bottle, and the pills spiraled across the floor. When he bent to pick them up, the pills he'd placed on my mist book tilted and crashed to the floor, intermixing with the others.

"It'll be fine. The two pills almost do the same thing. One changes the viewer's perception of what you look like, and the other one changes the pill taker into an ananoid. Not a big deal." He laughed. "Now back to your mission. As I understand it, you're to bring home Ralb, so your mother can finally have a decent night's sleep."

You'd think I'd be upset about that, but not me. I was a Zorcan. We can tell when someone is lying by his or her antenna. It grows! So there's no point in beating around the bush, if indeed we did have bushes on our planet. Another reason why I can't wait to get to Earth, I wanted to touch a bush. Pretty sad to travel through space, through black holes, and have as your goal to get pricked by a plant. You'd think I would have had enough with plants in the here and now. Oh, yeah, I guess I had one other goal. I know, I didn't forget. I had to find my stupid brother.

"So is this all I need? Zen said something about getting the T-gene."

"Personally, I don't think you're going to need it." He floated across the room, muttering under his breath. "One thing she doesn't need is more attitude. Must be those Earth genes hitting an overdrive button."

"Pardon me. Did you say something?" I heard him fine, but I wanted to know if he'd have the guts to repeat it.

"What?" he answered absentmindedly. "I was just talking to myself." He popped open another vial and turned it upside down, dropping the pill on top of my book. "This pill contains major attitude, so you should take it sparingly. You don't want to overdose on too much negative personality. It won't win you any friends on Earth."

What nerve! I did not have major attitude. I would have stomped my feet if I'd had them. However, I didn't want to make a fool out of myself. Besides, stomping your feet when you're wearing suction cups is more comical than anything else. When I got to Earth and had all the required parts, I was so going to throw a temper tantrum.

"But what do I know! Zen seems to think he knows all, so I'll leave it in his capable anaparts." He shuffled across the rock.

His ancient shell flaked and had an awful gray hue. His antennas were white, and his bottom eye was glazed over. A sure sign he was on his eighth eon. He wouldn't be long on Zorca-twenty-three. Probably looking forward to the afterlife. Rumor said it was filled with tree pots, a mawl's dream world. Xron read my mind.

"Yes, Oas. I am looking forward to my own tree pot. Can't say I know what I'd have in common with one, but I know there's one there with my name on her."

FYI—man, I love Earth talk—the people of that planet shorten everything. Anyway, I'd better fill you in, FYI, as to what it is. A tree pot is a heaven for an ananoid. It's your very own tree pot with leaves, fruits like berries, and apples all on the same tree. All to yourself, no sharing, no annoying brothers or sisters stealing anything from you. When you come from a flat rock planet with ten gazillion ananoids, the idea of anything with texture and something to call your own is your idea of peace. Doesn't take much to please us. Nor apparently others as well. Our tree pot colony is filled to the brim with deceased souls all enjoying eternal summer and bountiful fruits. We're open to all, except Edoricks. We have to draw the line somewhere. "So any idea what your tree pot looks like?"

Suddenly Xron seemed almost normal. Almost like someone I could even like. He took off his pieces of glass and wiped them on his spinneret. "Oas, I have to tell you. She's amazing. I have a telepathed snapshot of her. I'll project it on the rock wall over there. Look."

I stared at where he was pointing, and a fuzzy image appeared. Eventually it morphed into a sight I'd never seen before, and I'd seen my fair share of tree pots in the teleportation center.

"Well, what do you think? Isn't it the most beautiful sight you've ever seen? And she's mine, all mine." His eyes popped out even further than normal, and I was glad he'd taken off his pieces of glass because they would have probably flown across the room.

"Yep, she sure is different," I agreed.

"Oas, have you ever seen a tree pot so beautiful? Look at her. See how top heavy she is with fruit. Look over there at the size of the melons. I can't wait to sink my teeth into them. When I finish that, look at the strawberries. The branches are just falling with the lush, plump fruit. Then when I finish with the fruit, I can clean up with the leaves. Reach out and feel how soft they are."

He grabbed my antenna and jerked it towards the hologram. "I got to tell you Oas. The colony must think I was a star on Zorca-twenty-three because I've only ever seen a tree pot with those sized melons reserved for someone of the higher echelon."

"Well, you are a very special ananoid. I say lucky you and especially lucky her! Any idea when you're leaving?" I asked, rubbing my two mandibles together. I had stuff to do, and the asteroid I was supposed to be leaving on would be arriving shortly. I still had to say goodbye to Gorget.

I don't think Xron heard me, but I didn't have time to make pleasant conversation any longer. I needed some information.

"Is there anything I need to know about Earth?" I was willing to bow to his font of information.

"You'll be fine, just stay away from the popcorn and pizza," he said as he ran his antenna over his tree pot, seeming to forget I was even in the cave.

"What's popcorn and pizza?" I asked, suddenly afraid popcorn was going to jump up and attack me. Pizza sounded like something from Italy, a really cool country shaped like a flower having a really bad hair day. I'd have to have Rotsen fill me in on that one. Maybe he'd seen it on *The Sopranos*.

"People on Earth heat up kernels of corn, and

they eat it." He returned to his work.

"So it's food. I can handle food," I said, relieved it was only something humanoids ate.

"You teenage ananoids think you know everything." He turned and gave me a glazy stare. "Popcorn is too hard on our systems. We can't digest it properly. It's very salty."

"Salt I can handle. I swim in the salt water, and it doesn't affect me," I said.

He let out a sigh I'm sure Lehcarr, my BFF, could hear on her planet. "Oas, what am I going to do with you? Didn't you go to school?"

"I got the highest marks in my class," I said smugly. "My grades were even better than Ralb's." That wasn't saying much, but I did have a better attendance record as well, even before he'd high-tailed it off our planet. My bro was known for his creative excuses for missing homework assignments. His best yet was the dog eating his essay. That was really stupid of him because our planet doesn't have four-legged creatures unless you count the chameleons, and I don't even want to go there.

"Well, you must have been asleep the day they discussed salt particles. It's common knowledge salt in your present state doesn't bother you because you are ALREADY AN ANANOID." He calmed down slightly and returned to his normal high-pitched frequency. "If you have popcorn, it will change you from a humanoid to an ananoid."

I swallowed a lump in my throat about the size of a dodo bird's egg. "Wwwwwhat about pizza? What is that going to do to me?"

"Pizza is a very strange food. Technically it won't do anything bad to you, but be warned. You won't be hungry, but you'll still want to eat it. The aroma from a pizza gets right into your humanoid head and makes your mouth water." He continued bustling about. "The opening where humanoids put their food will drip."

"Mouth water?" I asked. How could something make my water in my mouth when it was presently so dry? Maybe I should just stay home and let Ralb fend for himself. He was a big boy, he'd find his way home sooner or later. Hopefully, much, much later.

"And I'll warn you right now—"

"Oh, no, what?" Could this get any worse?

"You won't be able to eat just one piece. It's very addictive." He flew over to his table that contained more tools and instruments than I ever remembered seeing. "When do you leave?"

"The next asteroid. According to Zen's math, it should be spiraling close enough for me to grab onto it in a moonlight," I said, trying to memorize the pizza-popcorn theory as well as all the other information he'd thrown at me. I should have taken notes. I knew I was going to forget something of major importance.

Xron flew over to the Edoricks and gave another deep sigh. "I hear that tree pot calling my name. My life is too short to spend it opening up Edoricks to see what they eat. Do you know, Oas, in the stomach of the one I looked at last eon, I found a hunk of metal with numbers and letters on it? I had to go on the *xobsetag* to even find out what it was."

Without waiting for me to ask, he continued, "A license plate for a four-wheeled dragonfly. Can you imagine trying to swallow metal? What was he thinking? I know they like anything shiny, but that's just plain ridiculous."

I agreed and while his back was turned, I grabbed an M burger in yellow wrapping sitting inside the *ptogher*, the rock where we heated up food. "When are you leaving for your tree pot?"

"I was hoping to depart next week. So I might not see you again, that is until you come to the afterlife."

"I'm only a youngster. I won't be heading over there anytime soon," I said, flicking my left antenna over my shoulder.

I planned to live long and be prosperous, as long as I stayed away from popcorn and pizza. Zorcans never get sick and never have any accidents. Thus, there are no insurance agencies on our planet.

"You teenage ananoids all think you're immortal. Will live to see six or seven eons. Well, I've got news for you. It passes a lot faster than you think. Just seems like one year you're on your first eon, then before you know it, you've lived eight." His gray antenna twitched and snarled like beacons warning me I should leave. I could take the hint.

"Alrighty then! I'll just fly out of here. I've got junkets to do and Zorcans to say goodbye to." I scampered over to the counter and backtracked my way out of the lab. Squeezing through the crevice on the way out was no easy feat. The stress of the trip had made me swell up like one of those puffer fish on Earth. I took a deep breath to calm myself. I didn't want Gorget to see me looking swollen.

Stars above! I forgot to ask him how I was supposed to get home. I rerouted my way back inside the cave and flew back into his lab. I coughed to let him know I was back and beheld a sight my three eyes will never forget.

I got there just in time to see him pull out a huge white box from the stomach of the Edorick. Xron held the box in both antennas and pulled. Streamers of cords and wires were attached. He flew to the other side of the room still holding the box, wires still inside the alien.

"Want some help?" I skittered over to his side. I set my mist book and telltale empty wrapper on the gurney and, with triads empty, prepared to assist him.

"Oas, you're back. How was Earth?" he asked

absently.

"Xron, I haven't left yet. I forgot to ask you something." I waited patiently for him to finish. But it appeared I was about to become his assistant.

"Well, ask away, but while you're asking, go over to that bloody idiot on the slab and grab the end of the yellow and blue wires." He lifted one of his suction-cupped anaparts from the floor of the Pod and stuck it onto the side of the counter. I assumed that was to give him more leverage for removing the item.

I did as I was told. To be honest, I was more scared of Xron than I was of the Edorick. I glanced inside his stomach. After seeing the inside of a humanoid, I don't know what I expected, but it sure wasn't what I saw. There was nothing there. Well, I should clarify that. What I meant was there weren't any organs, blood, or pulsing muscles. There was just junk. I guess he didn't have any room for his vitals with all the garbage he had in there. There were metal signs, inchworms, and even a girl's bicycle. This Edorick was a one-alien garage sale.

"What's that white box?" I couldn't resist asking, when I finally untangled the cords from around the bicycle.

"It's a humanoid *xobsetag*, or as they refer to them, computers. They are so underdeveloped on Earth. Look at how primitive it is. This huge box has half the information stored on it as you have in your *wad*," he said, shaking his head. "Now what was your question?"

"I don't have anything or any directions on how to get back here." I'd flipped through the book when my Parental Being was in the room with Zen, and I couldn't find any maps or compass points to help us find our way home.

"That's why you have to find Ralb. He has all the plans and navigation points. He has everything you need to travel back here. Now go!" He continued his work and, as I turned to say goodbye, I watched him pull out an entire set of books.

I retraced my flight pattern to the opening of the crevice and exited. Great stars! Now I really did have to find Ralb, if only to get back home.

Much as I was excited about my traveling, I dreaded the next few sunsets. I had to say goodbye to the ananoid who had finally noticed me, and it wasn't going to be pleasant.

Chapter Three

My *hanaglug* was filled with all I'd need for my travels. I had the pills from Xron in the side for easy access. One thing I'd learnt from asteroid travel when I went to visit my BFF—I loved Earthling-speak—was to keep air-travel sickness pills handy.

"Oas, there's a mawl here to see you. Oas has a mawlfriend, Oas has a mawlfriend," chanted another of my annoying brothers, Progri.

With one brother on Earth, you would think my troubles would cease. Not in my case. Not when you have as many siblings as I do. I don't know why my parents thought they had to populate our planet by themselves. It made dating really difficult. Who wants to date or kiss a relative? Major grossness.

I smoothed down my left antenna—it always stood up when I didn't want it to—and flew to the door of my crevice. As I got to the opening where my brother was waiting, I put the brakes on. I didn't want to look too, too available. My mother always says to play hard to get, to act like you're not interested. I had to bite my receptacle not to ask her when she played hard to get with my father—at number five hundred?

"Gorget, hi!" I flew over, and we greeted each other by briefly rubbing antennas, then intertwining them momentarily. I hoped Progri or any other of my five-hundred-plus siblings didn't see. They had a knack for showing up at the most inopportune time.

"Oas, what's this I hear about you traveling to Earth? I'm sorry, but I will not and cannot allow you to leave." He let go of my antenna, so he could look me straight in the eyes. His left antenna drooped over his middle eye, and I had to stop myself from reaching out to adjust it. He was taller than me, which was unusual, and slightly wider. He had the spinnerets of an ananoid who had built a lot of webs in his day. He worked with his father at the web factory, and he had the calluses on his pedicels to show for it.

But the best thing about Gorget, which made my heart flutter a mile a minute, was his bum. He had the cutest little tosh on Zorca-twenty-three, and it wasn't just my opinion. Lehcarr had thought so, too, when I'd asked her.

Looking me in the eyes, he leaned forward and took my antenna, in the way he knew drove me wild and crazy. My spinneret whirled in an unaccustomed way, and my antenna tingled.

He was cute, but surely he didn't think such a move would melt my corapeds or, even worse, make me change my mind. Cute butt or not, I was going to Earth on the next asteroid.

"What? You won't let me go? Excuse me, but I don't think it's up to you to decide if I go or not!" I was so mad, both my antennas and three eyes flapped about. I unraveled my left antenna that I'd hooked up with his and stood back, wings folded. I would have stomped my foot, if I had one. I was now going to have two temper tantrums when I hit Earth.

My brother Progri flew into the room. He sat back on his triads and pulled an M burger from under his pedicel. "This is gonna get good, and I have a front row seat."

"Go to your antechamber." Great! With my brother witnessing this conversation, it would be all over Zorca-twenty-three by the time the first moon rose directly overhead.

"You're not my mother. You can't make me." My

annoying brother spoke, food spitting out his eating hole. He continued to chomp on his food while he whipped a soda from behind his back, ignoring my words, but not my actions. They were being recorded in Progri-vision for all time.

"How much food do you have in there?" I asked, momentarily struck by the beverages he was consuming. Since the first soda, he'd brought out two more and was sucking nosily. He reminded me of the Edorick. With the amount of caffeine in his system, he was going to be peeling his suction-cup anaparts off the ceiling of his cave tonight. I sent a silent prayer to the stars above I wouldn't be around to witness the event.

"I'm a growing mawl, aren't I, Gorget? Do you want anything? I've got more food here, and I ain't going anywhere," Progri said as he settled into the spot in the cave.

I'd had enough of the mawl species in general. "Don't tempt me! I watched that Jackie Chan movie on my *gysogtom* last night. I learned some moves I'd love to try out on you."

"Okay, fine I'm going, honey butt. Just when it gets good, I've got to leave. In my next eon, I'm coming back as an adult ananoid," Progri said, as if we had a choice as to what or who we came back as. If I had my way, I'd be an only child.

"Let's go and take a fly," Gorget said in a soothing tone. "I want to spend some time with you to talk some sense into that little brain of yours."

Gently, he attached his antenna to mine. Again my antennas got tingly, but my spinneret remained calm. When he acted like this, he was the nicest mawl on Zorca-twenty-three. I don't understand how on one date he can be the biggest jerkaroo and then the next totally *jobeable*.

"Where are we going?" I asked, not really caring as long as I was with him. Maybe it was just his fear of losing me that was making him all nutso. Really! Mawls and their hormones. I didn't have time for his attitude. Stars, if Zen thought I needed a major attitude adjustment, he should spend some time with Gorget. Besides, I had an asteroid to catch.

It had been a long eon to get him to finally notice me. We'd been raised beside each other in the same air tank, where we had to stay until we were a minimum fifteen moons. It kind of takes away the feeling of newness when you've seen a mawl eat, sleep, and poop. But there was something about Gorget that made me sit up and pay attention. Maybe it was the way his antenna curved so neatly over his third eye or the way he beat Ralb at hearts and didn't boast, but instead winked his lower and middle eyes at me. It made my day and night and day.

He made my *jobe* bump faster. Nothing else and no one else on Zorca-twenty-three even competed. I didn't know what I had seen in Fronzy, because there was absolutely, positively no comparison. Gorget hung the moon as far as I was concerned. No really he did, the third one to the left of our planet. It was a tad crooked, but I wasn't complaining. Honestly, I thought it was pretty cool, and he was the best.

Until he told me I couldn't go to Earth.

On our first twirling of antennas, Gorget had brought me to a slot in the cement landing strip of the airport. I didn't want to think how many other mawlines he'd brought there. It only mattered that he'd taken me, and we headed there now.

Zorca-twenty-three is known—not that I'm bragging or anything—as the planet with the most evolved airport system in the galaxy Libra or Aries. It bugs my BFF Lehcarr to no end that her planet is number two. Which if you can't be number one, why bother?

We flew towards the airoport, ducking the dragonflies carrying the smaller of the species. I made a graceful landing, I must say, very delicate and feminine, my anaparts barely touching the ground. Gorget on the other hand landed like a stone. I hoped he didn't hurt his little tosh.

When he hooked my antenna and pulled me into our own special crevice, I thought I'd died and gone to the Neveah system. We backed into the spot, so we were both facing out, watching the dragonflies swoop and dodge. Their riders' vibrations of giggles created a feeling of butterflies flipping around my stomach.

"Oas, about this going to Earth," he began.

When I turned to look towards him, he focused on the largest of the dragonfly, his head weaving back and forth in time with the movements. He sounded nervous, but I had no idea why. It wasn't unheard of to travel to another planet. After all, our planet had populated the others. What? You thought you were the only planet with life on it? Get real!

"Gorget, no matter what you say or do, I have to go. I have to bring Ralb home." It was one thing for me to have second thoughts, but to be told I couldn't go? Well, I wasn't my mother's child for nothing.

"Why? You don't even like him." He flung one antenna to the front and picked dust particles out of it.

"Of course I like him. He's my brother." Okay, you have to say you like your family members, even if you don't. It's a cardinal rule. Not the bird. See, that's why I can't wait to get to Earth. I want to know what a bird is like, any bird. Can you believe my list? A bush and a bird, but just so you don't think I'm totally weird, if I happened to pass by Johnny Depp, I'd touch him, too. Probably more than once. He is the bestest-looking humanoid out there.

"Oas, it's me Gorget you're talking to. I know for

a fact you don't like him. You find him annoying and a pain in the anapart." Again he flicked his antenna. Hard to believe I found that attractive at one point.

"Gorget, what's the problem? Up until three eons ago you didn't want anything to do with me. Now you're upset that I'm traveling to another planet." I pulled the antenna out of his hand and forced him to look at me, with all three of his eyes.

"I *jobe* you, Oas. I've never felt like this before. I *jobe* everything about you, I think it's cute how your left antenna is slightly larger than your right one. I like how your eyes do a delightful little dance when you are really concentrating on something," he said in a deep monotone that sent quivers down my spine.

What? Was I dreaming? Hallucinating? Was the hottest mawl on Zorca-twenty-three admitting he *jobed* me? Okay, maybe he wasn't a movie star, but on our planet he was a pretty darn close.

Why did my life have to suddenly become so complicated? Maybe I should pass up space travel for a cave and five hundred offspring with Gorget. I shook my antennas to rid my *p-brain* of the thought. There was time enough for that when I was old, like my Parental Beings' ages.

"Me, concentrate? I think you might have the wrong ananoid." I laughed.

"I like how every time single time I try to get serious and talk with you, you flick me off like an annoying bug." He refused to look me in any of my eyes, just kept picking at his antenna.

Frankly, I was beginning to find it a little nerve racking. "No, the annoying bugs are my brothers." I smiled, my mouth curving upward, but my heart in turmoil. It was a sensation not unlike the time I ate three M burgers in yellow wrappers and then went on a whirly bird upside down. Not a pleasant experience.

"Well, I've got to tell you. I'm totally confused by this admission," I said, grabbing my own antenna and picking the dust particles off it. Funny how I found it annoying when he did it, but comforting when I cleaned my own. It was awful the dust and dirt you picked up from flying. Plus I hated it when my antenna dragged on the ground. Germs, yuck.

"So you'll stay?" he asked calmly, his lower eye flicking and flocking. If I didn't know better, I would have thought he had a dust particle in it, but I think he thought it was appealing. Mawl, he was nervous.

"I'll let you know." I had to get out of the crevice before I did something I'd regret for the rest of my eons. I had to get away. I had to talk to Lehcarr. She'd know what to do or better yet, what I should do.

"Wait!" he begged, down on all mandibles, his wings tucked in behind him in subservience.

This was a Gorget I wasn't used to, and I wasn't sure I liked. I'd had more fun when I had to chase him to get him to like me. Now he was giving himself to me on a skimming stone, I didn't know if I wanted him. Okay, even I had to admit I was fickle. But come on, there was an entire solar system out there, and I wanted to explore it all before I settled down.

I had just gotten curves on my main body parts. I didn't want to lose them to a swelled stomach and babies. I had raised my own brothers and sisters. I was now free and wanted time for ME.

Besides I was only a few eons old, too young to get saddled down with a wannabe. I wanted to explore and discover the real thing.

"I'll see you later." I called over my left spinneret. I had a heck of a lot of thinking to do and not much time to do it.

Chapter Four

You know you really have a BFF when her instincts are to eat you and she doesn't. Lehcarr is a Venus Fly Trap and is programmed to eat insects. Like yours truly.

We met when she was on an air flight that got rerouted to Zorca-twenty-three during a meteorite storm. It was a bad storm. The meteorite shower threw sharp ice pellets in the lanes of our flight paths. All dragonflies had to land on our planet, no matter what their original destination was. It wasn't pleasant. We'd gotten the air-raid siren warning just as her dragonplane landed. Hanging onto the back of the dragonfly for dear life, she'd rolled off and lay on the cement. Exhausted. Eventually, she'd pulled herself across the cement and made it into our airoport.

Airmada controlled the entire fleet of dragonflies. The airoport was floating five megatons above the surface of our planet attached with cables. Our engineers had designed it so it was able to withstand meteor showers and storms.

I had flown into the airoport to pick up Ralb (who had ventured to another planet to go partying, then clubbing) just as she was sliding up the revolving ramp into the structure. Not an easy feat for a Trap. She'd planted her leaves, brought her roots up to her head like an inchworm, and then repeated the process.

I hopped onto the conveyor belt and was alongside her in no time flat. I looked around for Ralb, but his dragonplane had been delayed due to the storm.

I sat in the chair to watch the monitors when I felt, rather than saw, her climb into the suction-cupped chair beside me, her traps searching left and right for some food. Her roots were sticking out of a bag that allowed her to move easily. She was hungry. And I was dinner.

She spied me, her trap senses in overdrive with the hunger pains she must have been feeling.

"Hey, you over there with the antennas and the three eyes. Would you mind getting me a drink of dioxide juice? I need a hit!" There was desperation in her tone, and she seemed to be on her last roots.

Now I have to admit I was young and naïve, but something about her urged me to help her out. I flew to the dioxide bar, then over to her. I hovered just out of reach. That's the thing about my planet. If you're not acclimatized, you're in big trouble.

She was in big trouble. She was on the brink of extinction if she didn't get dioxide. She couldn't move. The tiny hair-like feelers on her face quivered in our dry air. Normally I would be afraid, but I thought she was going to die.

With my left antenna, I handed her the tube and let her inhale the dioxide.

"Thank you! Now I need some nourishment and I know just what." Her pink lips opened, setting the trap for some innocent ananoid.

It wasn't going to be me.

"Anything else I can get you?" I asked politely, at the same time inching away, out of the reach of her trap.

"I need food," she begged, her voice barely more than a squeak.

"Didn't you get anything to eat on the dragonplane? That dragonfly had a large wingspan. I would have thought they'd have given you something to munch on," I said. I'd witnessed her dragonfly landing and, considering the ice it was dodging, he'd done a magnificent job of it.

"No, the interplanetary travel dragonplane I took was a discounted one."

Most of our better dragonplanes pipe in dioxide, so when you hit the different constellations, you're acclimatized and don't feel anything. Not Airmada. It didn't give meals or drinks.

"It was last minute. I had to fly, so I couldn't be picky."

"What do you want to eat?" I asked, wanting to help her somehow. When you have as many brothers and sisters as I do, it becomes second nature to mother strangers.

"Don't worry. I won't eat you, but that femawl over there looks like a tasty morsel." She pointed with her root and then sat up straight in her excitement.

I glanced over to where she was looking and instantly formed a beautiful bond of friendship with her. She was going to eat my worst enemy, Kaj Eiram. Kaj was the *bain* of my existence. You know the type of person who rats you out to any adult within eyesight and flirts with your mawlfriend. That was Kaj, the *bain* in my butt.

No doubt Kaj had come over to report to anyone who would listen—or care—that I was talking to an alien plant, but faster than you could say, "See you later, Kaj," she was history. Lehcarr swooped her head out, and the tiny hairs on her petal, which had seemed so lifeless a short time ago, sprang to life and sucked Kaj in. Nothing gave me greater pleasure than to see Lehcarr lick her lips and smile.

How could I not love the girl?

Anyway, since then, we'd been best friends for eons. Now I needed to call her to ask her opinion and to say goodbye.

I flew across two mountain ranges and landed

not so delicately on Deep Mawl's Rock, a rock we jump off to see how far we can fall before we chicken out and use our wings.

Settling back onto the rock, I shoved my antenna into my left eye and made the call. Surprisingly, it doesn't hurt to put things in our eyes. I would have to remind myself not to try it on Earth though. We have three eyelids to protect us, whereas from what I've seen, humanoids only have one on each eye. What a major *rap-off.*

"Hey, Lehcarr. How are things?" I asked, telepathing with my mind.

"Oas, when do you leave?" she asked. I could see her and, while the picture was a tad fuzzy, she was sitting in her oasis of greenery, lightheartedly snapping at a swarm of mosquitoes buzzing by. An inch worm wasn't safe either, as one minute it slithered its way across a red, dusty rock and the next Lehcarr chomped nosily while a tad of green liquid dripped down onto her left leaf.

"How did you know I was going to say goodbye?" I was astonished she'd heard the news, when I'd only just heard it myself a few hours ago.

"Your brother!" Lehcarr replied.

I waited until her munching quieted. When silence filled my earphone, I continued. "Progri is a pain in the..."

"Not Progri. Ralb. He telepathed and told me to tell you not to come. He says he doesn't need your help. He's fine on his own. He says for you to stay and keep Gorget company," she said.

I caught a glimpse of her in my mind. Stars above, I wished I could be as happy and satisfied as she was when I ate. For her a meal was an event. Me, I was content with anything put in front of me. I wasn't picky. Probably because I had so many siblings. There was only so much food, and if I didn't eat it, my sibs would.

My antennas took on a life of their own and spit out smoke. Who did he think he was? Ralb trying to control my life? Not to mention Gorget. In like this entire lifetime, he never mentioned the word *jobe*. In fact any words of *adornment* weren't in his vocabulary. Now all of a sudden when I was about to embark on the journey of a lifetime, he wanted to spend eternity with me. Okay, maybe I'm putting words in his mouth, but it didn't take a rocket scientist to figure out his motives were pretty selfish.

"I can see the smoke signals from here, and I don't think I like the words you're using, young lady." Lehcarr reamed me out in the same tone my mother uses. She held up her left leaf in protest. "Hey, don't shoot the messenger."

"How does he even know about Gorget? When he left, I was still drooling over Gorget, but focused on Fronzy. Did Gorget tell him that so I'd stay? Okay, that is so not cool." My antennas simmered from the smoke and formed boxing gloves. I was going to thump my brother big time.

"Calm down, Oas, I confess. I might have mentioned it to him. He is your brother. He cares about you." Lehcarr continued chewing. Then the inchworm inflected her digestive system with a humongous burp.

"What or who are you eating? I can't concentrate with all the chomping going on in my eye." I was steamed. It was just like Ralb to ruin what little fun I had. He didn't want me to go. Gorget didn't want me to go. Well, guess what, boys? I was going.

"Sorry. I'm eating another inchworm. They're very bony on my planet. I have a limit of one per day, but he was right in front of me, so I couldn't resist. I'll pay for it later. The stupid creature will keep me up all night." She released another belch. "Now getting back to Ralb. He wants to protect you.

He doesn't want you to fall prey to the people or race he's struggling against. Ralb is concerned for your safety. He's been sick the entire time he's been there. Thinks it might be something he ate. It's sweet that he wants you to stay here nice and safe," my BFF said, unaware she'd been totally hosed by my brother.

"What nerve! He's such a mawl. He thinks he should have all the fun, while I get stuck here on this stupid planet. Well, I've got a newspaper for him. He's about to have some company," I spat out. My antenna flew around like the propeller on a dragonfly. I was furious.

"Calm down, Oas. Put your antenna back in." Lehcarr yelled so loudly, I could hear her voice coming from the eyepiece lying on the rock. "Shouldn't you think things through first? Maybe Earth isn't the best place for you to visit. It didn't work out so well for Ralb. I mean, who wants to go through a black hole only to end up with traveler's diarrhea?"

"What do you mean? My brother has you so snowed. You'll be thinking it's going to be raining crustaceans next week. If you knew him as well as I do, you'd realize Ralb is down there having a party time. He's having fun learning all about Earth and humanoids while I'm stuck here. The only reason he doesn't want me to go is because he doesn't want me to *camp his style*. He has you so brainwashed, you can't even tell the truth from science fiction." I wished I had something to eat. I wasn't hungry, but I needed to de-stress. I could really go for an M burger in yellow wrapping right now or maybe three or four.

"What about Gorget? He doesn't want you to go, right?" she telepathed. Geeze, hadn't she been listening at all. She was worse than my femawl Parental Being, big time.

I sighed before continuing. "No, he says he *jobes* me. Can you believe it? I bet he's in cahoots with my brother to keep me here. You know what, Lehcarr? I'm going, and nothing and no one is going to stop me. So goodbye, dear friend, I'll see you when I get home."

I yanked my antenna out of my eye and stood abruptly. I was at the end of my antenna. My BFF wasn't any help, and Gorget was only adding to my confusion. At my wit's end, instead of heading home I made a major detour and flew over a rocky red, dormant volcano before skidding to a stop in front of a large water basin. It was known on Zorca-twenty-three as a liquid well, but to me it was my thinking spot. I skittered across the barren desert and tentatively dipped my left antenna into the cool diamond-clear water. It cascaded through my body. It massaged my heart and gave my pounding muscle a slight squeeze before heading down into my stomach. It calmed the butterflies and even relaxed my seven toes.

I stared down into the dark mist in search of an answer. On one antenna, I had Gorget who wanted me to stay by promising me the moon, but on the other, I had my restless soul, which was yearning for adventure and excitement. I had a third, which cropped out when I was ticked. It was growing like Pinochle's nose at this moment.

The major question to be answered was if I would be happy settling with Gorget when I hadn't experienced life.

Dang it! I was going. If he *jobed* me enough, he'd be waiting for me when I got back, and if he wasn't here when I got back, he wasn't worth wasting my time on anyway. With a renowned sense of purpose, I headed home to pack.

A slight breeze gusted across the glacial lake, so I flew home with relative ease. Good thing, too. I was too preoccupied with my decision to concentrate much on airborne velocity and wind currents.

I drifted through the doorway into our abode and headed straight for my spot. When you have as many siblings as I do, it's unheard of to have your own room. Except if you're rich like Kaj, may she rest in peace, or should I say in Lehcarr's stomach. I'd rather be poor than have a lot of *daves* the way her family did. They treated their unicells like dirt and made them work five eons at a time without a break.

I opened my *hanaglug* and added the pills to the mix.

Rotsen twisted his petals around inside of the case and gave me a leaves up.

"I'm counting on you to get us there safe and sound, sweetheart." He folded in one of his yellow dandelion petals and grinned. "See you in St. Louis."

"But we're not going there." I double-checked my directions to make sure I hadn't gotten them mixed up somehow. I was known for being challenged in that department. "Nope, I was right. We're going to a place called Bedrocktown."

"I don't care where we're going, but I'm relying on you to get us there and if you don't..."

I shut the case before he could continue. He was my bedtime toy but, stars above, a lot of times he was rock-hard stubborn. Plus he liked to hear himself talk.

I scurried into my special spot, right next to a small crack in the rock, which let in a nice cooling breeze and settled in. Hanging upside down, I closed all my eyes and turned off all my senses in an attempt to get a nap in before I had to go. Despite my attempt to sleep, something kept poking me in my eye. My antenna shot around the side of my head to stop the annoyance, but still it continued. When I opened my eyelid, my brother was about to jab me again.

"Would you stop that? I'm awake now. What do you want?"

"Sis, I'm begging you, don't come down here."

I sat up to get a better look at my sibling, and I realized something strange. He looked like me except, of course, I was better looking.

"Ralb, how come you're not in humanoid form?" I asked. Despite being tired, the curiosity woke me.

"You think you're ready for space travel, and you can't even figure out a simple communication signal."

I so had to head to Earth if only to punch him in his triad or arm or whatever he was using at the time.

"Excuse me, for breathing. So what gives? Are you not a humanoid?"

"You're excused." His annoying laugh jetted across the airwaves and made my antennas crawl. "I'm talking to you on a Zorca-twenty-three line, so therefore I'm in Zorcan mode."

"Oh." It made complete sense to me now. Hiding my crossed antennas behind my back, I relayed what he wanted to hear across the galaxy. "Okay, fine. If you don't want me to come, I'll stay here."

"I'm glad. Oas, one day when you're old enough and mature enough, then you can venture on a trip with the big people. Right now though, you should be content to play happily with Lehcarr and make goo-goo antennas with Gorget."

What a typical condescending brother. I don't care what he thinks; I was so going to Earth and beating him up.

"Fine, I'll see you when you get home." I signed off before he could utter another word. Ralb, you are going to get the shock of your life when your sis shows up and rains space particles on your parade. The partee time will be over, bro.

Blocking Gorget and all his issues from my head didn't work, so I gave up.

I brushed past my Parental Being, who was in the midst of feeding my siblings, and stormed into the room, grabbed my *hanaglug*, and flew back out again.

"Parental Being, I'm off. Where's my mawl P.B.?" I asked, taking in the domesticated scene of my family. It might be an eon or two before I saw them again, but I wasn't going to get sentimental. I wasn't going to pee from my eyes.

"Your father is working overtime at the hive to get some extra *daves* for a family trip. Can't you wait until he comes home?" She flittered around, first in one direction, then the other, as if she weren't quite sure what she should be doing or where she should be going. Funny, she'd acted the same way when she'd found out Ralb had snuck aboard the asteroid.

"P.B., you know how tricky asteroid travel can be. It's not like you can schedule a flight on a dragonfly and hop on. If I don't leave today, I'll have to wait another half an eon. Your precious son is waiting for me to rescue him." I was trying to be tough, so I wouldn't water my eyes. Maybe I shouldn't travel through space just so I could thump my brother. I didn't handle time change too well and who knew how many time zones, I'd be careening through. No, I wasn't going to back out. Besides, if my stupid sibling could navigate his way to Earth, for someone like me, it should be a *piece of carp*.

"Oh good, she's still here." My mawl P.B. flew into the doorway and dropped his metal luncheonware container on the dirt floor before embracing me in a tight hug. I was going to miss him. He wouldn't admit it, but I knew I was his favorite, or at least in the top ten.

"Oas, your other P.B. and I were talking. I don't know if I want you to go or not. Apparently your

43

brother has fallen into the grip of the worst humanoid known on their planet. I don't want to lose two of my children." She grabbed her tentacle and braided it with her other antenna. A sure sign she was nervous, even scared.

"Now Oas, listen to her. Space travel isn't easy on the system. Why when I went..." He stopped speaking and when I turned to see why, he was on the major receiving end of *the look*.

"You mean you traveled to Earth?" I asked confused. "You never talked about it."

"It was a different part of my life when I was young and foolish. I made the best decision of my life, though." He reached over and wrapped his antennas around my P.B.

Stars above. I hated it when they got mushy. Didn't I have enough siblings?

"P.B., I'll be fine." I went over to her and wrapped my feeler around her slim body as I untwined my mawl's from around her. "Besides what sort of trouble could Ralb have gotten himself into? He's only been there an eon." I didn't want to mention to her I'd talked to him only a short while ago, and he seemed to be a-okay. Knowing how my P.B.s thought, they wouldn't let me go if they had an inkling he was fine. Stars above, it was a lot of work trying to keep on top of all these ideas. Even my antennas were aching.

"I don't know. It's bad enough to misplace one child to that horrible planet, but I couldn't bear to lose another. Why, I watched their news the other night. I believe it was called CCN, and the wars, famines, and grief going on down there, it just made my skin crawl." She gathered the dishes as my brothers and sisters finished eating, then wiped them, ready for the next meal. She leaned toward me and whispered in my antenna. "Do you know they pay people, who walk on red carpets, to star in movies, and they have children without being married?"

"Now my little rock lobster, that was going on when I was there, and I didn't end up any worse for wear," he said, as he reached across the table and grabbed a leafy twig she'd set out for my siblings.

I needed to distract her. "Xron took a humanoid apart, and I even saw what was inside. It wasn't too bad, though it did smell pretty horrid," I said, mentally checking off in my head that I wasn't forgetting anything important.

"I just don't know." She pulled a Lehcarr and ignored what I said. "If I let you go, you have to promise me to stay away from any red carpets and, for stars sake, stay away from anyone or anything named Oscar."

I had to cover my mouth, so she didn't think I was laughing at her, when in fact I was. Oscar, yeah right. Why couldn't anyone understand all I wanted to do was see the sights, get my stupid brother home, and then come back to Gorget?

"Your mawl P.B. said the entrapment was set by the worst of the humanoids—a teenage girl," she spit the words out before leaking from all three eyes.

Okay, maybe I did have my work cut out for me. I mean, I have seen Earth television shows, and I know how teenage girls operate.

But they've met their match when they come up against a femawls from Zorca-twenty-three.

Bring it on.

## Chapter Five

If you are traveling from or to nearby planets, then you are at the mercy of Airmada. But for longer journeys, you have to hit an asteroid. Not the easiest thing to do. The math alone, trying to figure out the exact time and date, is enough to send me into a brain meltdown.

I had my mist page from Zen with the latitude and longitude degrees that showed when I had to fly toward the asteroid. It was all a matter of precision, and I only had one chance. One mawl I knew believed he knew all and told even more. I'm sure you have the type on Earth. He thought he could do it without Zen's mathematical skills. Well, he took a running fly at the last asteroid when it passed through our galaxy. He didn't succeed. He ended up smucked like a bug in Lehcarr's jaw. Good riddance, I said at the time.

Carrying my *hanaglug*, I flew to Interplanetary Space Airoport, a fancy name for an outcropping of rock where good head winds hit the planet. I have to tell you, I was nervous. Scared, in truth. I wasn't a seasoned traveler by any stretch of the imagination. I mean it's one thing to hop on a dragonfly and be somewhere in a little over one moon cycle, but to travel through different seasonal zones is a heck of a lot more nerve racking.

My mom seemed to sense my fear because she teleported into my head and kissed my two antennas. "You'll be fine, dear. Come home safely."

What? No mention of Ralb. Maybe she did care about me after all.

I searched frantically through my *hanaglug*, my antenna poking through my belongings looking for my Rotsen. I didn't travel without him. Woow, I found him. Tucked under my *gysogtom*. Okay, I was good to go. I squeezed him once, then twice, for good luck. My Rotsen had been with me since I was a *yaba*. I had it in my air tank from day one, and it was a part of me. Even if it was a *tootoo*, I didn't care. It was my *tootoo*.

So I waited on the outcropping with an odd assortment of ananoids. There were the dreaded centibugs, annoying unicell creatures being sent to Earth to get rid of the tree drubs. Amazing how that planet needs our planet to survive. I guess that's what we get for being their parent planet. Offspring never really get over needing their P.B.s.

I walked back and forth, trying to calm myself before my big adventure. My suction-cupped anaparts squished on the rocks with every step. I had to calm my nerves, or I'd be tossing the contents of my stomach before I boarded the rock. I needed some time to go back to my lake and have another soothing drink, but there wasn't time.

Calm down. This is what you wanted. You'll be fine, I chanted to myself. I tried to switch the focus off myself and onto my traveling companions.

Great! My first trip to Earth, and I'd have to share it with a trillion of the unicells. Not the type of postcard you'd want to send home to brag to your friends. I could just hear Lehcarr laughing now. I'd have to make something up, so it sounded more exciting.

My pedicel shifted, and I trembled. My stomach rumbled. I'd forgotten to eat. Oh, darn, too late now. I'd have to wait until I hit Earth. Maybe I'd be able to find one of those M burgers in the yellow paper wrappers like the ones I'd discovered on the Space Station. I had so many things to do on Earth, I hoped I'd be able to fit in finding my stupid brother.

A mawl's bark invaded my head. I jerked my three eyes up to see Gorget standing in front of me.

"So you're going through with this crazy idea?" He asked his antennas wrapped around his torso in a tense manner.

I nodded.

"If you're headstrong enough to go ahead despite my older and wiser words, then I can't promise I'll be waiting for you when you get back." He huffed and puffed, as his eyes blinked in a chorus of rapid movements.

"Gorget, if you can't be happy for me and let me go on an adventure, then I don't think I really care for you to be lingering around waiting." I was shocked I said that, but, although my heart was constricting in pain at the harshness, I couldn't take the words back. Then I realized I didn't want to. If he wasn't the type of mawlfriend to trust me enough on another planet, then it was his *lost*.

"Oas, don't say anything you're going to regret."

"Gorget, I believed you were special but—" I held up my antenna to stop him from commenting. "If you're going to cause a scene in front of all these unicells about a simple little trip, well, goodbye."

"Gorget, I'm waiting." An ultra-high-pitched squeaky voice drifted over to us. I didn't have to look to the source to realize it was Kaj.

"What's she doing here?"

"If you come back with me, I'll drop her in a second," Gorget said as he reached for my antenna.

"First of all, I thought she was deceased."

He shook his head.

"That weed of yours couldn't kill a fly," Kaj announced with attitude.

"You two-timing mawl." The antenna I had a hard time keeping under control at the best of times took on a life of its own. Before I could stop it, it smacked him across the face, leaving a slight mark on his otherwise perfect face.

"Goodbye, Oas, and I hope you find what you're searching for on Earth," he said the words over his shoulder as Kaj wrapped her torso around his and led him away.

My eyes didn't cloud with tears. Instead I felt a lightness in my *jobe*, which had nothing to do with my recently consumed water. I knew he was too good to be true, and the fact that he was two-timing me with someone he said was uglier than me made me dread to think of the lies he'd told her about me.

I was free!

I glanced down at the mist paper. The outcropping I was standing on vibrated. This was it. I grabbed my *hanaglug* in one antenna and wrapped it several times around the handle. I didn't care about losing my belongings, but I sure as heck didn't want to lose Rotsen.

A voice sounded in my head. *Prepare to fly. Take a flying leap and hang on. Grab the mineral sticking out closest to you and wrap all tentacles around it. It's going to be a bumpy ride. There's a lot of turbulence in the air tonight. Due to that, we won't be able to hook into the satellite system on Earth and show you the movie we'd planned. If you look over your pedicels when you hop onto the asteroid, you'll see the emergency exits. Since we will be flying through the Milky Way, there are oxogyen vessels under your holdings. The trip has been overbooked, so it's every alien for himself or herself.*

I shivered. It was now or never. I flew, then took a running jump and landed on board the asteroid. I clung to the iron-nickel material, finding a pitted groove to grasp. My triads were going to be stiff and sore in the morning. They weren't used to this kind of action.

I tried to remember everything I'd been told to

do, but I forgot one important aspect. I forgot to hook everything on so it faced the proper direction. I was now plummeting towards Earth at an estimated thirty-two kilometers a micro-eon. Let me tell you, it's not fun. My last three days food was hurled toward my upper regions. It would have been my lower regions, if I'd been hanging on properly.

Finally, I got myself turned around the right way. Just in time to hit the black hole.

Oh, stars, NO!

When you go on a trip, there's always the part you're dreading. Earthlings have Customs Officers who check everything to make sure they aren't bringing in something they're not supposed to. Well, that's our equivalent of the black hole.

I held my breath and grasped tightly. No one had to telepath into my brain to tell me to wrap my tentacles around anything that moved. There wasn't anything. Traveling through a black hole is like being sucked into a vacuum cleaner, except less pleasant and a heck of a lot darker. Don't ask how I know, but I do.

Around and around I flew, hitting the unicells spiraling and kaleidoscoping. When I opened each of my three eyes, the colors blended and bled together, like a rainbow I'd seen over the three moons last eon, but more vivid, more intense. Instead of being muted it was polychromic, the tints were neon pinks and greens interspersed with yellow.

A whirling and whizzing like the twangy string of an out-of-tune guitar vibrated through my head, jarred my teeth, and throbbed inside my body. I swallowed to keep down my stomach contents and made the mistake of inhaling.

Traveling by asteroid on a ship made of iron ore doesn't make for a pleasant smell. When it's spiraling through Milky Ways and dodging space junk, it was even worse. An oily, gassy smell was my companion for the journey. That's when I knew I was going to vomit.

I struggled to keep down the contents, but up they came. Thank stars, the asteroid righted itself, and when I barfed, it flew away from me.

The twisting, twirling, and rocketing through space as we hit another asteroid and veered off course slightly caused a major migraine to erupt in my head. Where were my pills? I needed them within reach, but they were in my *hanaglug* at the tail end of my antenna.

It seemed like forever I'd traveled inside the black hole, but in reality it was only five days.

The halfway point was the *changeling* area. I had to become humanoid, and the changes were beginning. I reopened my three eyes and found, to my dismay, I only had two. How would I survive with only two eyes? I needed my third eye. Oh, stars, this was going to be worse than I'd thought.

I patted my hair and grinned. I had a Peg Bundy hairdo just as I wished. I was going to be so hot on Earth, I'd be sizzling like a barbecue.

I hit the wall of the hole and careened onto the other side, which raised red welts on my new body. It was like I was in a pinball game, slingshoting from side to side, but when I touched my hair again, it was still in the same place. It was as smooth as a dragonfly's wing. The lacquer pasted on top of it held its shape. Hairspray wasn't advertised for space travel, but this brand sure kept its hold.

My body changed in ways I hadn't anticipated. The neon skirt I'd requested was a tad shorter than I would have liked. Either that or my walking sticks were extremely long. Again I touched my hair. Maybe I should have gone with smooth silky hair like on those haircoloring boxes, but it was too late to worry about that now.

What kind of person was I, to be traveling at

warp speed toward Earth, and my biggest concern was my hair? I ran my mandibles through it. What? I had fingers? I quickly counted my appendances and found I had five on each hand. No antennas! What would I do without the most important part of my body? How do humanoids survive without antennas? This was going to be horrible.

Majorly dreadful, not to mention just plain gross. I had been so excited at the spur of the moment decision about going to Earth, I hadn't really bothered to look at the mist pages describing the changes I would have to go through to become a humanoid. I was in pain. Imagine have your entire body ripped apart and then reassembled. Then times that by ten, and you'll have a slight idea as to what I went through.

Oh, stars, now the very worst part. I had big, bouncy, and somewhat curly—where it wasn't plastered down—hair, which my appendances kept getting stuck in, and no antennas.

How did Ralb survive?

When I find him, I am so going to kill him again! I wondered if I could kill him twice. Once for not wanting me to come. And then for getting into the situation that forced me to come after him. This was so his fault.

Oh, no! Just as I thought it couldn't get any worse, it did. Big time.

We were heading at mach five through the Milky Way. I tried to bend my humanoid shape to protect the main body parts, all the while hanging on for dear life. I struggled for a better grip on the wall of the asteroid. I was facing an uphill battle. Me against the rock.

I reached up to another handhold to get more leverage, but no luck. Too many unicells were hogging the good spots. I wasn't athletic, far from it. Apparently you have to exercise quite a bit to use your hands to pull up your entire body. I hadn't. The force of the dive suctioned me to the asteroid with my face jammed up against the rock surface. When I shifted position, a protruding piece of boulder jetted into my mouth cavity. My tongue tasted flint. Using all the force I had, I pried my head away from the slate. I shut my mouth before suction overtook my body again and cemented me to the rock.

Stars above, no one told me the trauma my new torso would go through on the way to Earth. This was not my idea of a good time. One side of my face was going to have some major rock burn. Do you know how long it takes to get asteroid marks off your face? I sure don't.

Now I had soreness and aches in parts of my body I didn't even realize I possessed. I wiggled the sticks protruding from the lower area of my body. I craned my head down to see why they ached so intensely only to discover a pack of unicells using my body as a harbor. The entire back of my carcass was covered with the lower echelons from my planet. I only hoped that once we landed and they flew off on their merry way, they would take their pains with them.

All in all, it was a trip not worth repeating, I didn't even want to think about having to travel home. Maybe I'd take up residence on Earth and take my chances after six months.

I could officially become an illegal alien and move to Mexico. I could manage there just fine, I'm sure.

Being a humanoid was awful. I so wanted to turn the rock around and head back home. I even missed bossy Gorget. Maybe he was right. Maybe I should have stayed on my pleasant, comfortable planet and hung out with him in the crevice. Right, but stupid Kaj was keeping my spot warm.

I wasn't going to go there, think that. I'd made

my decision and, right or wrong, I was going to stick with it. I'd find my stupid brother, bring him back to Zorca-twenty-three, and get back to my life. Who knew? Maybe this time next eon, I'd be Mrs. Gorget and the mother of my own herd. *Negetiatory*, I wasn't settling. If he was cheating on me before I was the Parental Being of his mawls, then he'd definitely do it after. A mawl doesn't change his scales.

Nope! I was young. I was single. I was going to see the world before I settled down the way my P.B. had. Besides, Gorget was history. I would never settle for a two timing mawl. No one should.

We hit a celestial road bump. We stalled to a stop. I took a deep breath and then pointed downward, headfirst through the ozone layer. Thank stars, I found a hole in it. Projecting downward, I finally righted myself, so I was pivoting feet first.

I opened one of my two eyes—stars, this was going to be a pain with only two of them—and looked over at my traveling companions. The unicell closest to my head was giggling, laughing, and having the time of his or her life. I reached around to grab it and shake some sense into it, but it darted out of my range.

This wasn't fun. We could hit another asteroid and smash apart. Then who knew where I would end up? With my luck, I'd be picking sand out of my antennas in some desert. From watching the satellite, I'd seen that little particles from asteroids always ended up where you didn't want them. I had no desire to drift along like a rolling stone in the middle of some war torn country. I had enough problems as it was.

We accelerated and careened through space. Despite the speed and the altitude changes my hair didn't move. I hoped I liked the style because I was going to be stuck with it. The idiotic covering I'd been wearing since I hit the black hole was not what one should wear for space travel. Of course, I'd picked it out, but the black hole clothiers should have ordered the proper clothes for my travels. The material kept jerking up over my walking sticks and revealing flimsy white cloth covering what the humanoids call their private parts. See, like my P.B. says, I watch way too much satellite.

We continued to dive through the system. As we passed through a field of cumulus mediocris, the water spray hit my face. I cringed when I thought what it was doing to my hair, even though I was getting a nice facial for free.

What was happening to me?

A few days ago I'd only seen hair on the satellite stations, and now I was obsessed with it. It was a cruel joke by Zen to order me up cement hair. When I got back to Zorca-twenty-three, I would have a serious chat with him.

That's if I made it back.

*Five minutes to landing,* a voice popped into my head.

What was a minute? I had no idea. Zorcans measured time in eons. I had no clue. Suddenly it happened. The asteroid lost its magnetism. I was flung free, thrown from the rock faster than Haley's comet.

I flapped my wings to break the fall, but I didn't have wings anymore. I had no antennas to grab onto anything, which might break my descent. I only had appendances, walking sticks, and a mop of hair.

I was in trouble.

Big time.

Jane Greenhill

Chapter Six

I braced myself as best I could and attempted a
dive. Unfortunately, I wasn't a swimmer—or any
kind of sportsperson for that matter. I shut my eyes
and prayed that Zen knew what he was doing and
that he wasn't playing some sick cosmic joke on me.

It didn't work. I pulled my walking sticks up and
tried to land in a cannonball position. As I said
before, I'm not athletic. My idea of exercise was
watching the dragonflies take off. Doesn't do much
for the pedicel, but when you live in almost zero
gravity, you don't really care about what you eat.

I hit the water butt first.

It hurt. Imagine getting a rooney at mach five.

Down, down, I went. I straightened my walking
sticks out once I hit the water. I opened my eyes
underwater and found myself surrounded by
tentacles. It felt like I was home. I reached out to
touch one of the green sticks waving at me and got
stung.

What kind of welcome was that? Welcome to
planet Earth; here, let me bite you.

Lids on the top of my eyes blinked, and I when I
reopened them, curls from my head bobbed in front.
What kind of hair spray can withstand an asteroid
ride though several black holes and dimensions not
to mention the mists from clouds but as soon as it
hits lake water disintegrates? To be honest I was
glad I hadn't paid good money for the product.

I brought my hand to my mouth. The prick from
the plant caused a small nick on a bone and the
muscle underneath throbbed mercifully. As I placed

my lips over the cut and sucked, the anguish subsided somewhat. The ultimate in multi-tasking, I attempted to suck and hold my breath at the same time.

My bare feet sank into mud, slush, and genuine grossness. Without another moment's thought, I crouched like I did when taking off for flight on Zorca-twenty-three. I springboarded from the muck and propelled myself up toward the top. The sacs inside my body, similar to the ones I'd possessed on Zorca-twenty-three, were in desperate need of being filled. I kicked my sticks to reach the surface, but something held me back, preventing me from reaching the top. My lungs constricted, making me fuzzy, weak. The lake around me darkened. Not only was my new body trying to swim, but my head swam with dizziness.

I felt around to discover what was holding me back. It was the dang plant that bit me. Its tentacles clung around my torso as if I were a lifeline. With strength a professional wrestler would be proud of, I used my shirt to protect my hand while I pulled its feelers off me. Before it could entwine itself around me again, I propelled up toward a faint light that sparkled on the surface of the water.

On my way up, I opened my eyes under the water and came eyeball to eyeball with a fish who, seemingly bored, released an air bubble and then swam away.

Unicells whirled and twirled in front of me, obviously unconcerned with their need for oxogyen. They jetted and jived in my sight line, then darted away, only to reappear. Frolicking, they reminded me of the carefree shrimp that Ralb kept in a glass jar at home.

The lack of oxogyen in my air sacs forced me to fight to the surface. Giving an extra strong kick with my sticks, I broke free of the water and hungrily gulped the oxogyen. Like a starving animal lapping up its first meal of the day, I drank in the gas, inhaling so deeply I felt the oxogyen cascade down to my toes.

After my third mouthful I coughed in rapid succession.

I was used to pure air, not the yuck these humanoids breathed. Actually, I guess it was "us humanoids" now.

For better or worse, I was one of them.

I struggled toward shore with a swimming technique I made up on the way. It evolved as I splashed my hands on and under the surface of the water while my sticks pumped against the water. It wasn't pretty I could tell, but it kept my head above water.

A weed attached itself to my sticks. Panic enveloped me. It yanked me down, determined to take me to its underwater lair. But I didn't travel mach five on an asteroid to drown. I jerked and kicked. I spiraled forward so fast, the tentacle ripped from its host. My appendances propelled my new body at warp speed through the water. I held my breath to keep the horrid water out of my mouth and kicked until I ran out of water. I skinned my outer covering on the bottom of the lake. I crawled out onto the stony shore.

Great! Why couldn't I have landed on one of those beaches I saw on the Discovery Channel? You know the ones I mean. They're covered with hot guys in tight little bathing suits carrying drinks with pink umbrellas.

Figures my brother would be in an area with hard rocks instead of soft, cushy sand.

Where the heck was I?

I ducked as a giant dodo flew overhead and dropped a white bomb on my hair. With a sense of dread, I reached up and patted my hair. The white goop from the bird sat smugly like a lotus flower on the side. A gooey, gross mess.

My hair, which had been so pretty and stiff when I'd left the black hole, now resembled the result of a horrific science experiment in Xron's lab. A mop of curls sprang from my head in gravity-defying spirals. Words I hadn't even known the meaning of on Zorca-twenty-three spewed from my mouth.

My Earth visit was not off to a good start. Liquid from my eyes dripped into the water hole where I was standing, causing ripples in the water. My insides churned like a parachuting maple key. I dropped to my knees and hurled the entire contents of my stomach onto the rocks surrounding the shore.

I didn't think I had anything left in my stomach, but I was wrong. I brought up a green, yellowy-brownish mess. I bent and emptied my air sacs.

I don't know how long I lay on the stones. I rolled over on my back and watched the asteroid fall from the sky. Funny to think I had beaten it down here. The oblong rock, which had been my ship down to this planet, fireballed into the lake. The wake ricocheted against the rocks. Water spouted like a waterfall. Waves on the opposite shore splashed across the stones. They backwashed as high as the tree line, flooding against the trunks before settling back down to where they had been.

The water around the asteroid bubbled and made an odd, gurgling sound. Then the lake smoothed out as if nothing had happened. Next an eruption—a burp, almost—rose from the confines of the water. The plant that had captured me reared its ugly head from the depths. It turned its green, diabolical head toward me. I jumped up and raced behind a tree. Like a large suction cup, the aqueous liquid pulled everything around it into a deep watery grave. In a matter of minutes, the lake returned to stillness, its secrets hidden in the soggy depths.

Trees in a variety of shades of green, the rich hues of emerald fluttering beside the subtle olive leaves, outlined the shore, their majestic, terra cotta trunks reaching into the clouds I'd just traveled through. I inhaled deeply—something I wasn't used to doing—and was relieved I didn't cough. The intoxicating perfume of dirt, evergreen trees, and wild flowers assaulted my nose. I sneezed three times in succession.

Even from my position on the other side of the lake, I could see the unicells propel out of the water and onto land, ready to do their jobs. I was preparing to do mine as well. I just had to rest first.

I lay on my back and looked at the sky. White puffs of cotton batten floated by. One reminded me of Lehcarr and, all of a sudden, homesickness overwhelmed me. My *jobe* felt as heavy as the asteroid I'd traveled on. I didn't realize I had any more water behind my eyes, but I did because it fell in a masterful waterfall. To add to my misery, the two holes in the front of my head dripped gooey liquid. Stars above, I was peeing out my eyes and my nose.

I had to get a grip, or I'd be dehydrated in minutes. Then I'd be forced to head into the lake for more of that yucky water.

I took several calming breaths and, keeping a weary eye on where I'd last seen the attacking plant, I relaxed for the first time since I'd begun this adventure. The thrill of the space ride had worn off. I just wanted to get my stupid brother and get back home. I even missed Progri.

The sparkling water enticed me. I crawled over to the pool. I grabbed one of the glittering pieces, which reminded me of diamonds on Zorca-twenty-three. When I picked it up, it wasn't. Only liquid. I must have been dazed from the ride. But where the rock had landed, there were sparkles. I shook my head, more than a tad confused, but bent to lap up the water, using my newfound triads as a cup.

The water looked clear and crystal clean, but it had an aroma to it like rotten dodo eggs. But I was dying of thirst, and I wanted to get the taste of yesterday's lunch out of my mouth, so I didn't have much choice. Finished, I stood on my wobbly sticks. I tried to stand like a pink flamingo I'd seen on television and fell against the rocks.

Red liquid oozed out of a scrape. I poured a bit of the water over top and bit my lip to stop screaming. Stars above, did it ever sting. It did dilute the red liquid a tad. Each of the joints creaked when I moved them. I closed my eyes and concentrated on sending a message to my brain. Reluctantly, I stood again on the sticks. This time I didn't get fancy or try any acrobatic tricks. Cautiously I put one in front of the other. I did it. I screamed—this time in delight. I was upright.

My extreme focus coordinated my movable sticks enough to do as I asked. I pumped my fist in the air, I was so pleased with my progress. Wait until I found Ralb and showed him how Earth-adjusted his sister was. I wobbled, before my walking sticks shot out from under me, and I landed on the rocks on my butkus. Thank stars, I had padding there.

I struggled to my feet, using a rock to assist me. I pulled myself up and tugged at my short skirt, which had crept up to an uncomfortable height. Taking baby steps, I let go of the rock and headed into the bushes. I needed something to chew on, a plant of some kind to clean out my mouth. Even though I'd had water, a different yucky taste remained. The lake water was gross.

My jaw ached, probably from the face mesh with the rock. I put one foot in front of the other and found I didn't need to hang onto the rock. The short triads on the end of my walking sticks appeared to do the trick. Standing upright, I hobbled over to the bushes and plunked myself down on the closest rock.

Movement attracted my two eyes. A small insect stood stark still on a green leaf. I shot out my mandible-stick, one of the ones with the five digits on each side of my torso. The insect hesitated, but then climbed from the leaf onto my body. It bowed its front sticks toward me.

How cool was that! This Earth creature thought I was a goddess of some sort and was actually honoring me. How great was Earth? I was getting way more respect here than I ever did on Zorca-twenty-three.

Shrugging my upper left body part, I smiled down at the little insect.

"My Earth name is April." The name rolled off my tongue and seemed right at home here. Reaching out toward the creature, I stroked it much in the same manner my P.B. rubbed my back when she was in the mood.

It gazed up at me with green, beady eyes, and before I knew what had happened, it collapsed in my hand, all four of its mandibles pointing towards the sky. It wiggled a tad and jiggled a fraction. Stars above, the creature was in the throes of death.

I was a murderer.

"I didn't do anything. What's the matter?" I asked, unsure if I should give it some of my medication to help it along. Great! I'd only been on Earth for a short time, and I'd gone from being heroine-worshipped to killing my loyal and faithful subject. At this rate, I'd end up before Judge Judy before the sun fully rose.

"Help us," a squeaky voice begged.

I looked around to see where it had originated and found it was from my insect friend.

"Wow, you can talk. How cool is that! I thought you were a goner." I reached toward him with my mandible and with a cautious touch I rubbed his belly.

"Please, I'm one of you, and our species needs your help." He lifted his head, and then flopped it down into the middle of my mandible, as if the effort was too much for his tiny body.

"What can I do to assist you?" Watching the Animal Planet might pay off after all. I wasn't sure if I'd be able to operate on something so small, but I could sure try.

"I don't know." He sighed and lifted his head before collapsing back down into the middle of my hand.

"How am I supposed to help you when you don't know what's the matter? One person can only do so much." That sounded mean and a little short-tempered, but in my defense I had major asteroid lag, my stick was oozing red liquid again, and I was a teenager. I think even Judge Judy would rule in my favor.

"You're the wise, elder one. You need to help us." Then his voice hushed.

A breeze rattled the tree leaves and caused a minor ripple across the otherwise clear as glass, but yucky tasting, lake, so I had to lean closer to hear his soft voice.

I felt like Dr. Phil. All I needed were a couple of comfy chairs and some television cameras, and I'd be all set. Instead, I took a *sympatric* deep breath and waited for his next words.

"Please, I beg of you, Oas."

Wait a cotton-gathering eon. How did he know my Zorcan name? I'd only mentioned what people on Earth would call me.

I leaned forward and glanced into his eyes. He blinked three times in rapid succession and then lifted his head a fraction of a millimeter. He opened his mouth. I thought he was about to speak when he released a feeble burp. If I hadn't been staring so intently at his facial expressions, I would have missed the slight nod of his head.

"I am Forzon, your relative." His voice strained as he spoke.

"But you've been gone forever." Stroking his back rejuvenated him, but as quickly as he sprang up, his weak body drooped back into my hand.

"Oas, you have to help us. We're dying out here, and I cannot figure out why." He emitted a little cough and spit up a bit of green, yucky fluid in my hand.

Impulse made me wipe the guck on my skirt.

Oh, stars. I just killed my relative.

In the spot on the side of my skirt were the remains of Forzon, his front mandibles tangled in a mess with his back. I picked up one of them, hoping I could somehow put him back together, but all attempts were futile.

I scooped out with my mandibles a small hole in the dark, smelly dirt and placed him inside. I laid some rocks on top, picking an especially pretty one for the top, one I thought he might especially like.

"Forzon, please forgive me for smucking you and squishing your little body. May you travel home to Zorca-twenty-three and spend eternity with a tree pot." Liquid dripped from my nose as I finished.

Stars above. I'd only been on Earth a short period of time, and I'd already killed one relative.

I only hope when I found Ralb I could keep my lethal mandibles to myself.

## Chapter Seven

Mentally I went through my list of things I wanted to accomplish while I was on planet Earth. Touch trees and bushes and meet a celebrity. My mother had made me promise not to meet up with Oscar, but a girl could hope.

Well, I'd seen the trees and bushes and, to be rock hard honest, they didn't really live up to all the excitement. My celebrity hunt better come through, or I was just going to have to write this trip off as one of learning and rock salt it up to experience.

Nowhere on my list had I written: rid the world of praying mantises. What had I been thinking? That was the problem in a nougat-shell, I hadn't been.

Just as I thought my day couldn't get any worse, something spiraled toward me out of the sky.

Fast!

It twisted and turned overhead, the ever-shiny metal catching the sunlight and blinding my two new eyes.

I ducked and dodged, but I wasn't quick enough.

Clunk! My *hanaglug* hit me square in the middle of my hair holder. Sitting up, I tried to rub the soreness away, but it didn't work. Maybe the airsickness pills Zen gave me might help this throbbing. It was worth a try. I unsnapped the case and searched for them. I don't know why I bothered to pack so everything was in its proper place. It was a mess. The inside of my *hanaglug* reminded me of the body cavity of the Edorick. In the disaster area somewhere was my Rotsen. After shifting aside

Zen's pills, a hairbrush, and bandages, I found him. Safe and sound. No worse for traveling five days on a rock to another completely different gravity system.

Though he looked a little ticked.

"Wow, that was quite the trip!" Rotsen said with a New York accent. If you think I watch a lot of satellite television, you should see this leaf ball. He didn't attend interplanetary *loohcs*, instead he just lazed around on his pet rock and zoned out to the A and E channel. Unfortunately he was a unicell, which only enabled him to get one show on one station.

"Whatcha looking at?" He tossed his dandelion yellow petals over his stem with attitude.

"Great stars! I was hoping you'd leave your *Soprano* imitations on Zorca-twenty-three. I have enough troubles right now without your two centipedes thrown in."

A manmade craft propelled itself across the water, a humanoid on wooden planks tried to catch the vessel, without much success.

"Hey, babe. How's about a trip to a beauty parlor? You could use some fina tuning." His stem was intertwined around my pill bottle, and as I picked it up, I intentionally twisted him backwards. I knew I looked a sight and, frankly, I didn't need this rude dandelion telling me what I already knew.

"Hey, sweetheart. Whatcha think you're doing? If I wanta face that way, I woulda faced that way. Come on, Oas, be nice," he whined in a nasally voice, even more poorly imitated than his New York Italian accent.

"I have a headache and need some pills." I twirled him from around the outside of the bottle and tried to remove the cap. "Push down and turn."

"Having trouble?" Rotsen asked from the inside of the *hanaglug* where he'd landed. "It's childproof."

"Very funny! Tell me how they can send us to

different planets in entirely different solar systems, but they can't make a lid come off easily?" I had asteroid lag, and the last thing I needed was grief from a two-bit weed.

"Want me to try?" he asked in a sickeningly sweet tone to get on my good side, but it wasn't going to work. I was too smart to fall for his tricks. Heck, when you have as many siblings as I do, you were leery of anyone trying to be nice.

"What I want you to do is— Rotsen, what's that noise?" I paused, my headache and grouchiness forgotten as the air filled with the sound of humming and an off-key song by a hard rock band.

"Humanoid voices, I think," he whispered as he twirled his stem around my arm.

I panicked, and my forehead beaded with drops of water. I didn't want to meet humanoids in this manner. My hair was a mess, my clothes were too small, and besides, I'd just killed my relative. If the television shows I got on my *wad* were any indication, humanoids didn't take too kindly to murderers.

Great! Instead of meeting anybody famous I'd be sharing a jail cell with someone named Butch. However, there are quite a few bigwigs in the slammer. Before I could further develop that thought, the rational side of my brain kicked in.

"Oh, no, people are coming. What to do? What to do?" I fluttered around and jolted one way, then the other. I darted behind a fallen tree trunk only to find I was sticking out more than I was getting protection. With my mandibles flapping as if I were being attacked by a swarm of mosquitoes, I jumped up in major stress mode.

"Calm down," Rotsen said with a condescending voice. Any other time I would shoot him a dirty look for that.

Now for once I was grateful he was calm.

"Hide over there."

Gathering up my *hanaglug* and Rotsen, I hurried toward where he was pointing, but I wasn't fast enough.

## Chapter Eight

"My mom wants me to get a summer job, and I'm like it's so not going to happen." A girl about my size and shape plopped down onto the stones and leaned against the rock that Rotsen and I had hidden behind.

"That is so unfair. Why do moms always ruin everything? I mean, we only get one summer, so we don't want to spend it working. That's for, like, old people." I peeked around the rock mesmerized as the second humanoid sat down, folding her long walking sticks into a twisted mass of bones. The girl then picked up pebbles and threw them into the lake one at a time. The plop of the gravel accented each of her sentences.

"I know. She doesn't have a life, so she doesn't want me to have one either," the first girl said. "Nicola, I really want to get to know that new boy better, but I can't do it behind the counter at Licketty Fingers."

I poked my head around the side as she reached up and pulled off a grass-green tree leaf, ripped it apart, and flicked it onto the stones.

"Gross, who wants to spend their whole summer dishing out ice cream? Besides, it's freezing cold in that place, and Little Paulie is just plain creepy. I heard from Helena who heard it from Michelle who heard it from Katie that he came on to Trish. He's like ancient, and that's just plain icky." For emphasis she reached up and this time ripped off three leaves at once and angrily tore them apart.

"Suzz, do you really believe that? You know how

Trish lies. But I agree. Little Paulie is so uncool."
Nicola stood up and used her mandibles to wipe
stone dust off her butt. She crouched behind the
other girl and began to braid her hair.

"Hey, Little Paulie's on *The Sopranos*. I might
get to meet someone famous," Rotsen whispered, but
not quite quietly enough.

"What did you say, Nicola?" Suzz twisted around
to speak to the girl whose fingers were flying
through her hair.

I ducked back behind the rock and tried not to
breathe. You'd think I'd have an easy time of that,
since I wasn't really used to having such big air sacs
to begin with, but nope. Today had gone from bad to
badder, and I hadn't even left the lake.

"I didn't say anything. I've been braiding your
hair and listening to you rant about not working.
There, done." The girl gathered up another handful
of stones and tossed them one by one into the lake.

"I'm so not hearing things. Someone said
something, and if it wasn't you and it wasn't me,
then who the heck was it? Do you think the new boy
followed us here? I know he really likes me," Suzz
bragged as she joined her friend tossing stone pellets
into the lake. "I could tell. He kept fingering my hair
like he'd never seen anything so shiny or clean
before. It was kind of weird, but kind of nice at the
same time."

"You'd better get up there and say something. If
they find you hiding back here, they're gonna think
you're an alien." Rotsen poked me with his stem.

I resisted the urge to give him a good swat.

"You, idiot, I am an alien," I whispered back. I
tried to get the words out, but I'd been holding my
breath for so long, my face ballooned outward, and I
couldn't help myself. I needed some of the dreadful
oxogyen in my system. I started coughing.

Oh, stars above. I couldn't catch my breath. I

was going to die.

Goodbye, any celebrity I might have met. Sorry, cousin Forzon for ending your life so suddenly. I was going to a hot place down below that had nothing to do with warm sunny beaches.

"Put your arms up in the air. It'll help get air back in your lungs," Rotsen yelled in a voice that mimicked mine.

"Okay, I heard that. Who's back there?" the girl with the nasally voice ordered.

The one called Nicola stood up at the same time I did, and we both did what girls do.

We screamed, the sound echoing across the bay, so it came back two-fold toward us. If I weren't so creeped out, I would have thought it was kind of cool.

"Stop it! That hurts my ears. Where did you get such a high-pitched scream?" she asked me.

She covered her ears, but not before I saw two shiny gold rings attached to each of them. Wow, how awesome was that! On Zorca-twenty-three, it was common to put a circular disc through the area above your eyes, but never through your ears. That's where your *wad* went. You couldn't risk damaging the sensitive organ.

I patted down my hair, which was standing up at all angles. The girls seemed about my age, but I could brag about the fact they were both shorter than me. Yep, I was the tallest. Thank you, Zen. He'd gotten something right.

I grabbed my *hanaglug* and held it protectively in front of me. I wasn't sure about the custom here. Zen hadn't gone into the day-to-day workings of a humanoid, just that I had to find Ralb, so I was on my own. I didn't think it was the right time to bring out my mist book. I didn't want to have to listen to the ear-piercing scream again. So I'd do what I would have done on Zorca-twenty-three, I'd watch and learn.

"Why did you scream?" she asked, flicking one side of her hair behind her gold-hooped ear.

The one called Nicola had hair the color of a flame. I reached out to touch it. I'd never seen anything that red before unless you counted the sun, which was kind of a reddish-orangey tone. But when I saw the strange look on her face, I quickly withdrew my hand. I was impressed that when I thought of something in my head, the rest of my body followed suit. Almost like playing *Follow the Leader*.

"I was sleeping when I heard voices. I hid behind the rock because I didn't know who was coming," I said, as I observed the two females.

Nicola was wearing a tight shirt with a word I couldn't pronounce on the front and even tighter jeans. I glanced down at them and wondered how she ever got them done up.

The other girl Suzz was dressed much the same way, except her short-sleeved top was green, about the same shade as the vomit I'd projected out, but I wasn't about to make the comparison to her. The manner in which she tilted her head to the side so her hair hung at a perfect ninety-degree angle made me realize she was the Kaj of this planet. I had a hard time reading the words over the bumps that stuck out from the front of her shirt.

When I looked down at my torso, I was surprised that I had the same kind of bumps. How strange I hadn't noticed them before. Without a second thought, I reached my mandibles across my torso to squeeze my orange-sized balls. I happened to glance toward the girl named Nicola, and her mouth opened in shock. My mandibles dropped to my side, and instead I reviewed the attire of the femawl named Suzz. If it were possible, her pants were even tighter than her friend's. I peered around the back of her and saw a strip of pink material sticking up from the back of her jeans. I wanted to tell her they were falling apart, but thought it might be best to mind my own business.

"You were sleeping on these rocks. Are you crazy? Don't you have a home?" The second one stood up from tossing the stones and hiked up her pant coverings. She stared at me and then glanced away.

When I opened my mouth to say I came from Zorca-twenty-three, Rotsen slapped me on the back of the leg with his petals.

Right! I had to think of something fast. I couldn't tell them I came from a planet and traveled via an asteroid at a speed of mach five. They would think I was crazy. I thought I was nuts, and I knew the truth.

I had to remember I wasn't dealing with the most intelligent species on the planets. Humanoids after all, were afraid of Edoricks. I had to improvise, make something up. When in doubt, stick to lies that are close to the truth. Ralb taught me that. He should know. He was either in trouble or caused more dilemmas than someone on *The People's Court*.

"I came to find my brother. He ran away from home. He called to tell my Parental Being...er...I mean my mom, he was okay, but she wanted me to check. To make sure he was okay. You know how moms are when it comes to their little boys." My torso had a mind of its own, and my shoulders shrugged. "She wouldn't care if I ran away but, stars above, if something should happen to her precious little boy—" I paused to catch my breath, crossing these strange, short sticks at the end of my mandibles, hoping I hadn't revealed too much information.

"That is so true. My brother can do no wrong and, like, I can't do anything right." Nicola held her fist out.

I had no clue what to do with it, so I hit it with my fist. I tried not to pummel her too hard. My mandibles should be registered as deadly weapons. They'd already taken one life, and I hadn't even spent one night on the planet.

"Sisterhood forever!" she said as she nudged her hip against mine. This was a weird ritual. I just hoped it was a good thing and that she didn't have a pot of boiling water to drop me into.

"Sisterhood forever!" I repeated, feeling quite proud of myself for fitting in with the sisterhood, whatever that was.

"So I'm Nicola, and this here is Suzz. Her name is really Suzan, but she thinks it's too common. So she goes by Suzz."

I held out my fist again for the sisterhood chant, but it was duly ignored. I guess sisterhood only went so far.

"I'm Oas, I mean April. I'm April Oas," I said, glancing down at my clothes and comparing them. They lacked big time compared to the ones my new friends wore.

Despite what my mom said, I had to watch more television. I was so behind the times it was pathetic. I had to find out where these girls shopped. I had to dump my skirt and change my hair. Apparently, puffy hair was out, and razor-sharp with streaks of pink and yellow was in.

I had so much to learn.

"That's really strange. We've only had one new boy in town recently, and his last name wasn't Oas. If it was your brother, wouldn't you have the same last name?" Suzz asked, the right digit of her mandible poking me in the upper torso.

Right away, I could tell this girl was going to be a problem. I would have to keep my feelings about her to myself, though. If Rotsen found out how I really felt, he might have her erased.

"We had different fathers. In fact, my mom doesn't know who his father is." Hah, that would fix my P.B. for giving me so many brothers and sisters.

Stars! I just remembered in the mist page Zen had given me humanoids were semi-monogamous. They liked to stick to one person when they were married. Unless they were Mormons from a long time ago, but I really didn't research that far back.

"Hey, you are a member of the sisterhood." Nicola jutted her fist out again. I guess I passed whatever it was I needed to satisfy membership into their club.

"I have no idea either who my father is." Suzz shrugged. "Nicola is the only one I know of who knows for certain who her mother and father are. How boring is that!"

I looked over at Nicola and a wave of sympathy erupted from my heart all the way to the middle of my face. I had just met the femawls, but I didn't like how this Suzz was picking on her. It wasn't her fault her P.B.s *jobed* each other and stuck with each other through thin and thick. Nicola turned bright red. I don't think it had anything to do with the proximity of the golden globe or, as humanoids called it, the sun.

Zorcans have a saying, keep your friends close and your enemies even closer. I was going to have to be glue stuck to this Suzz.

But I had other things I had to do first. I had to find Ralb and save him from the clutches of the evil teenage femawl.

"So what did the new boy look like? What was his name? I need to know if it's my brother, or if I have to search another town for the dweeb." I hastily tossed Rotsen into my *hanaglug*, much to his displeasure.

"Why did you just put that ratty old dandelion in your suitcase?" Suzz asked.

I had to hold it tight, because Rotsen had heard her comment and was thrashing about. He'd turn into dandelion wine, if he didn't watch out. Either that or he'd take a round out of Suzz, not that I'd stop him after how mean she'd been to Nicola.

"Um, nothing. I just thought I'd help clean up the junk around here and pick up weeds. Personally, I can't stand the things. They make me sneeze and are extremely bothersome." I fumbled around and tried to act like I was one of the cool teens.

"What do you think you're doing?" his muffled voice screamed as I attempted to close the *hanaglug*.

"Shhh! I don't want them to think I have a talking plant. They'll think I'm nuts." I struggled to close the lid, but he wasn't having any part of it.

He gave up whispering and telepathed the message to me. "If you don't listen to what I have to tell you, you're crazy. Suzz, the femawl—or as they call them on this horrible planet, the girl—over there is trouble. She's going to be a stone in your shoe."

"I know. I have things under control. I'll let you out as soon as I can. Now behave." I whispered to him. I shuttled the two parts of the *hanaglug* together and used the mist key to shut it, keeping my back to the girls, so they couldn't see what I was doing.

Finally successful, I stood up. "Okay, now how do I get to your town? Can you point me in the right direction?"

"Oh, we were just leaving," Nicola said. "We'd be more than happy to show you the way. I'm starving anyway."

"Your hair is really cool," Nicola said, as she walked beside me. She reached up and ran her fingers through my mess. I was amazed her sticks didn't get caught in it. It felt worse than a spider's web, and it probably had space junk in it.

"Really,' I said, more than a little astonished at the sincere tone in her voice. "I was thinking how nice yours looked."

"I'll take you to my hair salon as soon as we hit town." She linked her arm through mine.

"You don't want to look identical to Nicola, though. I think we should try something diff with you," Suzz said, as she tried to look over my shoulder to see what I had behind my back. "I could visualize you with gel and mousse."

"Probably be best to let my hairdresser decide. We don't want you to end up with something too wild and crazy," Nicola said firmly.

"I'll be with you guys in a sec." I unlinked my arm. "I just want to make sure I haven't forgotten anything."

When I glanced around to make sure they weren't looking, Suzz was picking a leaf or something out of Nicola's hair, totally absorbed in her actions.

Hoping I still had some of my alien powers, I shook the *hanaglug* twice, and it folded itself into the size and shape of a piece of chalk. It was small to begin with, but I really didn't feel like carrying it. I hoped my new friends wouldn't notice.

When I held it in my hand, Rotsen's movements jerked the sides back and forth as he bounced off the walls. He was snarky, but he'd just have to suffer for now. I'd make it up to him later. He had a weakness for chocolate bars and, from the dimensions of Suzz, she would know where I could find one or ten.

I tucked the chalk into one of the pockets in my covering and followed the girls away from the lake. I glanced back over my shoulder to see if I could see the asteroid, but it must have been at the bottom of the lake. I brushed a tear from my eye. Shoot, I didn't want my eyes to pee, but I was leaving the last part of my Zorcan life in that water reservoir.

What was I going to do? I had to find Ralb. I would worry about everything else later. For now I had to join the sisterhood and find my darn brother.

But first and foremost, I had to do something about my hair.

## Chapter Nine

We walked through the woods. Or rather I should say the two girls strolled like a couple of runway models through the woods, whereas I stumbled along behind. In my defense, though, it wasn't like Suzz and Nicola had space traveled today. But who knew a place that had all kinds of tall trees and bugs would have such an uneven floor? I mean, come on. Is it really that difficult to smooth it out? As soon as I picked myself up after falling over a tree root, I tripped over a log. If I heard Suzz ask me one more time if I had a nice trip, I was going to pull her eyelids off by the base. I realize now how horribly violent that sounds, but on Zorca-twenty-three it's what you do to your annoying little brothers. And I should know, I have enough of them. Brothers, that is—not eyelids. I really missed my third eye, especially when I could decorate it the way that Nicola added paint to hers. It was an amazing shade of cocoa.

"Be careful what you wish for!" Rotsen's voice telepathed into my head. "You wanted to touch a bush and now you have. One thing you can cross off your mist page. HA, HA!"

Do you know how much I wanted to take that piece of chalk and draw something really rude with it? But I didn't. Not because I was trying to act all humanoid, but because I didn't want to explain to Suzz what I was doing or why.

I touched the leaves on the trees in wonder. No two were the same. How can one planet populated by the likes of my Uncle Forzon, may his soul *rest in pieces* have so many amazing things? A tad slimy, yet smooth, and the little veins that reached toward each tip reminded me of tiny vessels of life. Reluctant to set it down, I counted the points before my attention was caught by the next piece of foliage. Growing right beside it was an evergreen tree, its sticks and branches prickly to the touch. The scent of pine and its outdoorsy freshness filled the holes in the middle of my face, which Rotsen telepathed to me with an extremely deep sigh, was called my nose. When I was sure Suzz wasn't watching, I licked the green leaf first. It was wet with a tinge of a mint taste. It was a long way from an M burger in yellow wrapping, but not too bad.

The evergreen needle pricked my tongue, and I yelped. Suzz seemed to think it was due to some forest creature I'd encountered, so she sighed and continued on.

I ventured through the woods, a smorgasbord of tastes and smells. I ate a red berry, which I immediately vomited, tried a blue one, and kept it down.

"Anyone want a piece of gum?" Nicola asked as she pulled a package with little white bumps out of one of her pockets.

I was impressed she could squeeze her hand into her pants to remove anything.

"Hold out your hand."

I wasn't quite sure what she was talking about, but I followed Suzz's example, and she plopped a square-shaped item into my hand. Like them, I put it into my face hole and moved my jaw around.

A burst of strawberries tingled my mouth, and it felt really enjoyable, even if my already sore jaw was getting a workout. Why the heck hadn't they ever brought gum to the Space Station? The substance didn't dissolve or even reduce in size. I followed the girls' example and kept moving my jaw, but my mouth dropped open, and the gum fell out as Suzz blew a bubble. I bent to pick my piece up from the dirt when I caught Nicola's eye, and she gave her head a little shake

"Hey, Nicola." I had dragged behind the others, "What is that odor?"

Deep in the woods, far from the amazing smells of the wild berries, sweet wildflowers, and musty moss alongside rich, fragrant dirt was a cloying smell hostile to my new nostrils.

Nicola stopped, and Suzz let out a sigh that, even from my short time on Earth, I knew was one of annoyance. "What are you talking about?"

"Don't you smell something odd? Something that isn't normal?" I asked as I stopped and ran my fingers over the bark of a tree. These fingers were good for something, and I couldn't believe how sensitive they were. I thought my antennas were touchy-feely, but the tips of these appendages were something else again.

The covering of the tree trunk was rough in spots, while in others it appeared to be smooth, almost worn down. Small round holes pierced the bark in no particular order, and I almost asked another question when a small bird flew to the top of the tree and began tapping another hole.

"Well, it could either be the smell of the sulfur bubbling up from the bottom of the lake or that animal carcass rotting in the bushes," Suzz answered. "Now can we go? I have to be home in twenty minutes or my mom will have a hissy fit."

I followed the strong nauseating scent. On the other side of a medium-sized boulder lay the entrails of some unknown animal, open for all to see. Sickening as it might sound, the sight reminded me I hadn't eaten since I'd left home. I wasn't a cannibal, but I could just imagine the glances I'd get from Suzz if I bent down to gnaw on that. Still, it made my stomach rumble. I'd better find an M burger fast, or I might start biting these shiny, clear, half-moons on the ends of my fingers. They must have a purpose. Suzz was munching on hers, along with the gum, probably because she lacked proper food.

"Are you a cannibal?" I asked, nodding toward her chewed parts.

"Very funny." She snorted, reminding me of a pig and not in a pleasurable, yummy, bacon way.

Finally after what seemed like eons on Zorca-twenty-three but wasn't even a full moon setting we reached a clearing. I had just gotten used to walking over tree roots. Now a different dilemma faced me. Where once there were trees and roots, now the ground in front of me was a dull gray. Beyond the two girls a bright yellow line stretched along the middle of the cracked and smelly path. We had tar at home, but we never thought to harden it for racing strips. I would have to take notes, so I didn't forget anything. Knowing Ralb he wouldn't use his fact-finding mission for anything important. I dreaded to think of the items he'd remember when he got home. Probably how to make popcorn and pizza, and we know how popular those two items would be at home. He'd end up killing off our entire race. I kept my balance by placing one foot ahead of the other until I came to the end of the yellow line.

Nothing! The line ended and then it started again. I did what I thought was best. I jumped. I ended up on the second yellow dash. Stars! I'd have to jump again. I bent down on my walking sticks and prepared to jump. I was swinging my mandibles in the air when suddenly I was grabbed from behind.

"Are you nuts?" What are you doing in the middle of the road? You're going to get yourself killed!" Suzz screamed in my ear. "Then you'll never find your brother."

A loud blast sounded close to us. She dragged me off the black tar and onto the gravelly pebbles beside it.

A dragonfly with four wheels sped by. It was shiny, red, and big. Larger than any dragonflies on Zorca-twenty-three. Heck, it was almost as large as the asteroid I flew here on.

"Sorry, I guess I wasn't thinking," I stammered. I had to learn to follow and not lead. That way I should be able to survive these four-wheeled dragonflies.

"Can we get a move on?" Suzz grabbed my arm. I could tell it wasn't out of love or caring. I think she just wanted to make sure I didn't get killed on the way to town. I don't think she was worried about me. Probably just didn't want to get grief from her mom. Maybe we did have something in common.

I stuck to the gravelly part and walked directly behind the two of them. We passed a large green sign with white lettering up on stilts.

"Bedrocktown, Florida. Pop. One hundred and sixty-three," I read aloud. "Bedrocktown. Isn't that where Fred Flintstone lives? I thought cavemen were extinct."

Suzz rolled her eyes at Nicola. "We live in Bedrocktown, not Bedrock. Fred Flintstone was a cartoon. He wasn't real. What planet are you from?"

I felt the chalk twitch in my pocket. Stars! Rotsen knew me better than I knew myself. He knew I was about to tell them what planet I was from, and it wouldn't be a pretty sight.

I thought I'd change the subject, but it only got worse when I asked the question, "Wow, does everyone get pop in your town? Do you really have one hundred and sixty-three varieties of pop?"

"Suzz, she's trying to be funny. That's a really good joke, April." Nicola laughed. "Are you originally from Canada? They talk so funny up there. We call it soda here."

"That's right. I was trying to be funny," I confirmed, hoping she'd forget about where I was from. I had no idea what I was trying to be funny about, but I'd give it a try. I would do anything for the sisterhood.

The trees swayed, and leaves danced in the slight breeze. I wished when I'd gone through the black hole, I'd been given a sweater. My mom warned me about Canada, but she didn't say a word about Florida. I hated it when my arms got cold. Probably had something to do with the time I was out drooling over Gorget and my wings froze.

Nope. I wasn't going to go there. Gorget was my past. Suzz and Nicola were my future. He'd be sick of Kaj and no doubt waiting when I got home, but I was having zip to do with him. I wasn't going to waste my time on a fickle ananoid.

I rubbed my arms and, when I looked up, I was relieved to see a building. Finally, we were getting into Bedrocktown.

Bedrocktown with its one hundred and sixty-three varieties of pop was bustling. The first building we reached at the top of the hill was a pretty stone structure with painted windows and a big cross on the top. I guessed that was so you could find it in the town. Beside it was a place with walls you could look through. Inside numerous tables sat scattered in no apparent pattern around the room. I cupped my mandibles around my face and pushed against the glass to cut down on the glare. Stars above, they weren't attached to any cables to hold them in place. Situated at each of them were *gilders* filled by humanoids. The *gilders* seemed a tad small because the bottoms of their torsos were overflowing the edges. Garbage littered each of the tables—an array of cups alongside half-eaten M burgers without the yellow wrapping. Some humans held

little white vessels up to their pedipalps with their
littlest finger sticking out. A trick I would have to
learn. If I ever got any spare time.

"I'll see you guys later. I have to go home." Suzz
looked at the two of us, and then did the strangest
thing. She put her baby finger and other mandible
up to her ear and mouth and said to Nicola, "Call
me!" I have to give these humanoids credit. I didn't
think they knew the first thing about mind
telepathy, but I guess I had a lot to learn.

Now that Suzz was gone, Nicola and I walked
side by side along a white cement ribbon in front of
the buildings. One building with those see-through
walls had lots of books, and the pages didn't even
look misty. How odd was that!

"Here we are at my salon. Let's pop in for a
minute and see if Damon has some free time so he
can get you fixed up." Nicola pulled open the door,
and I walked through.

I stopped, trying to absorb all the action in front
of me. At seven different pods, men and women sat
in black chairs, their hair being pulled, combed, and
brushed into a variety of gravity-defying styles.
Harsh noises assaulted my ears as the sounds of
seven small handheld vacuums blew the hair in
different directions. When I tore my eyes away from
the sights, I glanced down at the floor and found
tidbits of the same hair sprawled around. Trying to
make a getaway from the evil machines was my
guess.

"Damon, there you are," Nicola addressed a man
who was her height. He wore a black apron. In fact
everything on him was black, save for his bright
orange hair. "I have a friend here who just arrived in
town, and I was wondering if you could fit her in."

"*Mon dieu*," he said, picking up a strand of my
hair and dropping it as if it contained bugs. "I was
about to have my lunch, but obviously this is an

emergency."

"Thank you, Damon. I owe you." Nicola pushed me toward the back of the salon.

"Luciana, I need a wash back here, pronto," he screamed so loud I covered the side of my head.

He glanced at me and shrugged his shoulders. "I have to be heard over the sound of the hairdryers."

A girl materialized beside me and gently led me toward a bowl. Pushing me down onto the chair, she tilted my head backwards and sprayed water at me.

I jumped up and got ready to thump her the same way I do my pesty brothers, but Nicola shook her head.

From her facial expression, relaxed and smiling, this must be the norm. I settled back down and let this water demon do her squirting. This Earth was one crazy place. On Zorca-twenty-three, we didn't have to go into a building to get wet, we just headed down to the local watering hole and waited for the geyser to erupt.

With a towel wrapped around my head, I was plunked down into Damon's black chair, and he wrapped me in a big piece of material that reminded me of a vampire's cape, except it covered my front instead of my back. I loved those old scary movies I watched on my *wad*. I swirled around so I could look in the mirror. Other than my eyes poking out from under the towel around my head, an upturned nose, and a small budlike mouth, I looked just like all the other female Earthlings.

Damon turned me away from the mirror and, with the quickness of Edward Scissorhands, he gave me a new haircut. Nervously, I looked out of the corner of my left eye as I saw him stirring a variety of small containers filled with goo. Long wands protruded from each. I cringed as he decorated my hair with the goop. He painted bright purple and white on the strands, then he placed thin pieces of silver under the colors and folded them into squares.

My stomach felt as if I were hovering on an asteroid, as if a thousand butterflies were doing the limbo inside.

I glanced toward Nicola. She must have sensed me looking at her, because she removed her gaze from the glossy magazine she was reading and smiled. She stuck her thumb up in the air, which I guessed was a good thing. It must be a secret sign for the sisterhood.

I watched the black hands of a clock move around and, just when I thought everyone had forgotten about me, Luciana came back.

She led me over to the water fight place again and removed all the silver.

"Sit back and enjoy the massage. I'm going to add some shampoo and conditioner to your new mop."

Soapy suds cascaded down my neck and dripped onto my back. I jerked upright at the ticklish sensation of the water hitting my skin. The spray nozzle she had in her hand flung itself around the room like Rotsen when he was ticked about something. Only it was squirting water every which way.

I jumped up out of the chair and swatted the mouth of the beast. I tried a karate chop move I'd seen Jackie Chan use, but it didn't do anything. Well, it did, but I don't consider hitting the hair-washer girl in the face with the hose a successful move.

Finally, she took control of the situation and thumped on a piece of metal beside the sink. It silenced the monster. We all took deep breaths. At least I did.

I surveyed the damage caused by the monster. Water dripped overhead, cascading in a waterfall to the floor.

"What in heaven's name happened here?" Damon stalked over. He looked angry. His arms were crossed, and he held a razor-sharp knife as if he planned to do someone some harm.

"It was the hose." The girl grabbed some pieces of fluffy material to wipe up the floor, but she wasn't quick enough.

Damon turned and slipped. He reminded me of a skater and not a very good one at that. His arms flailed about, and he jerked and jived like Ralb did the time he was attacked by a swarm of honeybees. Damon reached out to grab the chair, but it spun around.

Smack! Down he went onto the floor.

I glanced over at Nicola. She was covering her mouth, but smiling. I didn't think it was funny, but then my Earth sense of humor isn't fully developed yet.

Glowering—and, yes, I know what that look is— he pulled himself up with his hands, using the chair for leverage. I guess he forgot it twirled around, because when he put his weight on the back of it, it spun around like a weed in a tornado. His face flushed red, and he reminded me of my P.B. when Ralb came home after curfew with his breath smelling of dandelion wine.

I was about to help him, but Nicola grabbed my arm and held me back.

When I'd first entered the salon, it was noisy and bustling. Now it was so quiet you could hear a *pincushion* drop.

Damon got to his feet. My eyes were drawn to the back of his pants, which were wet and covered with my hair. When he'd fallen he must have ended up in the pile of discarded tresses trying to make a getaway.

"Get her hair washed, towel-dried, and get her over to me." When he got to his feet, he placed his upper mandibles on his back and bent over backward. The expression on his face was that of a very unhappy camper. And he wasn't even camping.

The girl who'd been washing my hair pushed me—and I must say she wasn't too nice about it either—into the other chair. I cringed when I heard the familiar pulsating water. But this monster seemed more in control than the other one. I was washed in no time.

"Your hair is dry," she muttered as I felt more liquid hit my head.

How could my hair be dry when it was soaking wet? I thought about mentioning to Damon that she didn't know what she was talking about but decided to say nothing. I wanted to get out of here as soon as I could. I didn't need to encounter any more monsters in one day. Stars above, the evil plant in the lake had nothing on the creatures I experienced on dry land.

Like a magician Damon arrived behind my chair and, with the handheld vacuum, he began pulling my hair. I screamed and whipped my head around like I was possessed. I don't know if he was getting back at me because he fell, but I wasn't going to take any grief from him. I was a Zorcan—the superior of the races. I wouldn't let this mawl attack me!

As I was about to hit him with an evil stare, I caught a glimpse of Nicola. She had a look on her face that rivaled my mother's when she didn't like what she was seeing.

Immediately, I dropped my hand, brought it up to my silky soft hair, and grinned at Damon. "Sorry," I said, hoping the five-letter word would convey my true feelings.

My pocket jerked out and in like a humanoid's heart. Rotsen was miffed because he was missing out on all the action. I reached down and flicked him, making a move I knew particularly annoyed him as I took my frustration about Damon's hair-pulling out on the plant in my pocket.

"Voilà." Damon spun me around so I could see myself in the mirror.

"Wow, you look fantastic with bangs," Nicola said as she came and stood beside her hairdresser.

My former Peg Bundy do had been replaced by a straightened, lightened-up version of the girl who graced the cover of the magazine Nicola had been leafing through. It was shiny, shimmery. I reached up to touch it, and the strands felt softer than anything I'd ever fingered, including the leaf.

"April, you look like Paris Hilton." She grinned. "Wait until Suzz sees you. She's going to be as green as a chrysalis with envy."

"So I did good?" Damon asked, smiling as if he already knew the answer. From the look on his face and the sound of happiness in his voice, I think I'd been forgiven for his fall, even though it was the water monster's fault and not mine. Honestly, maybe now that he'd seen how the sleeping giant could act when provoked, he'd get rid of it.

"Damon, you're a miracle worker. How much do we owe you?" Nicola asked, her tone serious.

Rotsen shifted around in my pocket. When I put my hand in to shush him, instead of touching his little plant-like petals, I found a wad of paper money. I withdrew my mandible and silently handed the bills to Nicola.

I glanced between Nicola and Damon, crossing my fingers I'd handed her enough. Apparently, by the smile on Damon's face, all was okay.

"When you come back in six weeks for a touch-up, the visit's on me," Damon said, pocketing the money faster than Rotsen eating an M burger with yellow wrapping. Really this guy should join a traveling fun fair. People would pay big money to see his disappearing act.

Six weeks? I hoped I wouldn't be here six days, but to be honest, I could get used to all the pampering.

With a wary glance over my shoulder at the water monster, which was now creating havoc on another poor unsuspecting soul, I followed Nicola to the door, and we headed outside.

I inhaled the scents of the town. Beside the hair salon was a store selling loaves of fresh bread. An older femawl entered the store and squeezed the loaf displayed in the front window. Her fingers made indentions in the bread and then the dents disappeared. Wow, it was magic!

Pulling myself away from the temptation of the grains en masse, I walked past and then stopped suddenly. Behind the see-though glass was a pair of jeans identical to the ones Nicola was wearing, except these were on a pair of walking sticks.

Stars above, someone cut off the rest of the body. I grabbed Nicola's arm and pointed. I stood on the tips of my walking sticks to search for the red ooze that had flowed from me when I scraped my knee on the rocks, but there wasn't any. Probably it had happened a long time ago, because all the guck was gone.

"Where's the rest of her body?" I asked my sisterhood as my new hairstyle blew in the rustling breeze.

"You just crack me up." She laughed. "It's a mannequin."

"I knew that." I thought I'd better change the topic before she decided I was an alien. "Would you mind if I tried them on?" I asked, not wanting her to think I was copying her or anything, but she did look good in them.

"Are you kidding me? I'd love to take you shopping." She pulled me through the door, setting a little bell tinkling overhead. It reminded me of a little chorus of bird songs. Then I frowned and looked up as I remembered the white mass that had ended up on my head.

"Mary, this is my friend, April, and she needs some new clothes." Nicola headed over to a rack of clothes with the words "New Arrivals" on a sign in big orange letters.

"Grab a changing room, and I'll bring these in for you. What are you, like a size two?" she asked as she flicked her hair over her shoulder. I tried to copy her move and ended up spinning around in a circle. Oh, well, in my spare time I'd have to work on doing that without hurting myself.

I wasn't quite sure how to grab a changing room, so I stood behind her as she pulled clothes off the rack. Then she headed into a little room with a blue dove-soft curtain.

I removed the skirt and slid on the jeans, which were the same design as hers. I had to suck in my stomach and not breath too deeply, but I got them done up. I turned around to see what I appeared like to someone walking behind me, and I looked good.

I flipped my new hair over my shoulder. I tried to remember how Nicola and Suzz strolled in the woods. I teetered and tottered before I got the hang of it. I glanced at myself in the long reflecting mirror and with the confidence built into the jeans, I did it right. Guess I just needed to practice a bit as I strutted in front of the mirror.

Whoever this Paris Hilton person was, she had better look out because April was in town and she was smoking. Okay, I wasn't really smoking, because it's terrible for you, but I looked pretty darn hot.

Nicola poked her head in. "I knew those would look good on you. Try this shirt on, and we should be good to go."

I put on the T-shirt she brought for me and

struggled to get it on. It was tight. Very tight. I pulled it down over the orbs that stuck out on the front of my chest.

"Could you get me a bigger size?" I whispered to Mary, who was hovering outside the curtain.

"That's the way all the girls are wearing them these days. Your friend looks good, Nicola," Mary said, flinging the curtain to one side.

"April, wait until the boys in town get a look at you." Turning to Mary, she said, "Can you dispose of her old clothes? She won't be needing them."

"Wait!" I squealed, and grabbed for my old clothes, obvious panic in my voice.

The two femawls turned towards me, surprised.

"I have to take everything with me. I can't leave without my, ummm, wallet." I took the pile. "I'll just take them with me. I feel kind of attached to them. You know, memories and all."

"Of course, I'll just cut the tags off your new clothes, and we can ring them right up." Mary flounced over to the cash register.

I rooted through the pockets of my mini skirt and grabbed the essentials. Rotsen handed me another wad of bills. He was the best banking machine ever. Better than those holes in the wall I saw on my *wad*. I paid for my clothes, and then treated Nicola to a shirt she was fingering.

She stood in shock as I grabbed it out of her hands, gave it to Mary, and then gave her the bag. "This is for you to thank you for all your help in making me fit in."

She squealed and then leaned over and kissed my cheek. I was getting the hang of making friends on Earth. It was fun.

Mary put my old clothes in a bag like Nicola's, and arm in arm Nicola and I strolled down the street. An alien and a humanoid in search of a good time or at the very least something to eat.

\*\*\*\*

"Want an ice cream cone? My treat and I'm not taking no for an answer," Nicola said as we got to the last building in the row. This one was really strange. It wasn't made out of bricks or even straw (like in the three little pigs story). This one was made of metal. I know because I knocked on it, and it pinged.

Nicola held open the door and, when I went through, a burst of cold air hit me. I hate cold air. See my Parental Being was right! I should have taken a jacket, and I don't even think I was in Canada. The Canadians must freeze.

But I forgot all about the cold, for what I saw made me awestruck. Behind a wall you could look through were bins and bins of different colored frozen liquid, all with different names, really weird different names. There was Strawberry Asteroid, Vanilla Shooting Stars, and Chocolate Galaxy. The glass was misted a bit at the front and a tad cloudy. I have to admit I had a twinge of homesickness in my main body cavity. The titles of the products, though, made me feel like I was in a home away from home.

"Where am I?" I asked confused. Rotsen thumped in my pocket. He probably wanted to be released, so he could see what was so interesting, but I didn't care. It didn't even bother me that Nicola looked at me like I was, well, an alien. I had to ask.

"Boy, you must have come from a small town if Licketty Fingers has a big variety of ice cream. They only have ten flavors here. Over in Middletown, they have a store that has ninety-nine different kinds." She grabbed a ticket from a red machine and stood in line behind a group of mini-humanoids. Their faces were pushed up against the glass, their breath causing small fog circles.

"Whatcha want?" a pulsing voice called from

behind the glass. My head jerked up at the fierceness of the tone. I wasn't used to deep voices. Xron had the deepest voice on Zorca-twenty-three, and his voice had been known to break glass.

I peered up at a mawl without a strand of hair on his head, discs that protruded out each side at ninety-degree angles, and a stomach filled with a large balloon.

This voice was so low it sounded like it was hitting the floor. I shivered more from the meanness of his voice than from the cold, but that wasn't helping either.

"I'll have vanilla. What do you want, April?" Nicola asked, obviously not intimidated by this man.

He bent over and flicked water off a small metal scoop. I braced myself for another water bath, but surprisingly he managed to keep control of his instrument. Maybe Damon could learn a thing or two from this mawl. He reminded me of a green monster from the movies, except he wasn't green. His bald head, despite the coldness of the shop, was beaded with sweat. It was gross, especially when it dripped into the ice cream. I was sure glad he wasn't scooping out mine. Nicola had been looking the other way, ignoring but also sneaking peeks at a gaggle of mawls in the corner. I'd have to learn how to do that trick, look at someone, but ignore them at the same time.

The guy handed over her ice cream and then glared at me.

"I'll have the chocolate one." One of my covering slits shifted. I'd have to save some for Rotsen. He loved chocolate. On Zorca-twenty-three, you could eat all you wanted and not gain an ounce. Life was great in space, but I was soon to learn it was not so hot here.

Freezing, in fact.

I was struck speechless when the man came

around from behind the counter to retrieve a dollar bill from a jar marked "Tips" on the counter. What is it with these humanoids? Why did everyone expect a tip? Even Damon thought he should make more than his set price. When it came to our turn, I was going to give him the tip of wiping his head before he leaned over the ice cream. Anyway, he turned around and bent over. I didn't want to be rude, but I couldn't help but stare. He was falling apart. He was splitting in two. I'm not making it up. Right where his pants ended, I saw two mounds of flesh, and they were split in half.

Of course, I felt sorry for him. How awful! I would order a large to help him pay for his skin operation. I wasn't sure what it was called, but for sure he needed one.

"Are you sure you want chocolate?" Nicola whispered. "Doesn't it break your face out?" She scratched her own face. "I get so many zits when I even look at the stuff. I guess with all the freckles on your face though, you don't have to worry about a few more spots."

"I didn't even think about zits," I said, rolling the unusual word around in my mouth. "You pick for me."

"Little Paulie, she'll have the vanilla," Nicola said, with confidence.

She took a plastic spoon out of a box on the top of the counter and then stuck it in the top of her cone. I watched her dig into her tight jeans and pull out some crumbled paper. Earth bills. I was about to jostle Rotsen to have him hand me some, but she gave him enough for me as well. I don't know how she got herself into those jeans, never mind a mandible with five fingers. But then she'd managed with the gum, so maybe they expanded inside. That must be it. Another trick I'd have to learn. I'd have to make a list so I didn't forget anything else.

I grabbed my ice cream, as it was called, and copied Nicola. Cautiously, I stuck my tongue out and licked it. The vanilla taste enveloped my taste buds. Yummm. For someone who didn't like the cold, I was in love with this cool treat.

I was a teenager. I was allowed to be fickle. Poor Rotsen squirmed and shifted inside my covering. He would be lucky if he ended up with a drip.

"Hey, who's the new chick? She looks pretty hot." A mawl leaned one of his mandibles against the back of a red plastic seat and stared at me. I'd watched enough Earth television to know he was one of the cool kids on the planet. He wore a way-too-big-for-him baseball cap, the brim of it straight. Brown curls erupted around the edge of the hat and fell to his shoulders. He had curly brown hair that fell over his two eyes—how weird was that to see someone with two eyes—in much the same way that Gorget's antenna fell over his three eyes. Funny how I spent all the time at the hair salon to have my hair straightened out, and his was curly. I guess that was one of the differences between the mawls and femawls of this unique planet.

I glanced over at him and shrugged. Showed you how little he knew if he thought I was hot, when in fact, I was freezing.

"Is she your cousin, Nic? You two have the same color hair," another voice called from the group of mawls over in the corner.

What on Earth was he talking about? Nicola had beautiful hair, which flowed down her back with the coolest rainbow of colors I'd ever seen. Damon had worked wonders with mine, but it was still nowhere near as lovely and amazing as hers.

"Just ignore them," Nicola advised me, even though she was looking at the tallest one over the top of her ice cream. I guess on planet Earth that meant come over here, because that's just what he did.

He strolled over to us wearing shorts that fell off his hips and, while I wasn't looking on purpose, I think I could see his undergarments. I wasn't sure that's what they were, but there was plaid material showing under the shorts. Well, at least his skin wasn't cracking like Little Paulie's. He wore a T-shirt with a big white check mark on the front. I assumed it meant he'd passed something or other.

A rock the size of Gibraltar, which I saw on an educational channel, filled my throat as he came nearer.

Rustling in my pocket proved Rotsen was awake. Stars above, I knew he wouldn't let the Little Paulie comment rest. I knew the frigging dandelion would want to see for himself if the ice cream man was a *Soprano* wannabe.

Before I could stop him, he wiggled his way out of my *hanaglug* and shot his petals out of my pocket. I pushed him down inside, but he fought against my hold. With a renewed sense of strength, he stuck his head out and flopped it around like a humanoid watching a tennis match.

"Settle down," I hissed.

"Why do you have a weed in your pocket?" the mawl asked.

"I'm into saving the environment," I said, thinking on my walking sticks.

"Cool. Hi, Nicola, who's your friend?" He looked me up and down, over and out. I wanted to run, but strangely, I was stuck where I was.

"Hey, Josh, her name is April," Nicola said, then stuck her tongue out and lapped at her ice cream cone. Next she dipped the spoon into the ice cream and turned the spoon upside down before putting it in her mouth. I knew if I tried it, I'd have ice cream all over me.

I looked up from my ice cream and into the

brownest orbs I'd ever encountered. They were deeper in color than any tree trunk I'd ever seen. My entire being seemed to be suction-cupped to the floor, but that was impossible. When I glanced up into his face, my stomach somersaulted. It wasn't a one-time occurrence. It happened again when I peered around my ice cream at him. I have to admit my stomach did a little flippy-flop. I'd never felt this way with bossy Gorget, or Fronzy either.

I pretended I had ice cream on my hands as they were sweating like mad, and I had to wipe them off on something. This mawl created feelings in me I'd never encountered either here or on Zorca-twenty-three, but I liked them. More importantly, I liked him.

"April, huh. Where you from, April?" he asked, again starting at my head and looking down to my sticks, then back up again.

I don't know what it did for him, but, to be honest, it sent shivers down my spine, and it wasn't from the coldness of the ice cream. That much I knew for sure.

"She's not from around here," Nicola answered for me.

Boy, was she speaking the truth. Just as well, because I had just taken a mouthful of ice cream. Besides, this mawl was making me speechless.

I no sooner placed a hunk of the cold ice cream in the center of my eating hole than I experienced a sudden, excruciating pain.

My head was going to explode. I thrust the ice cream cone at him and clapped my mandibles on either side of my head to get rid of the lightening bolt of agony charging through my brain. But they were useless. Nothing helped rid the inside of my head of the mind-numbing ache.

Xron had warned me about pizza and popcorn, but he hadn't said anything about ice cream.

"Brain freeze!" Nicola said knowingly. "Sit down in the booth and take deep breaths. It'll be gone in a minute."

She was nuts. There was no way this suffering was going to evaporate any time soon. I would spend my Earth time with a megawatt of a headache. This throbbing sensation wasn't going away. I saw stars and not in a good way. In the background I heard Nicola and this boy talking. They didn't seem worried. Help! Aren't there doctors on Earth? Can't they call one? Humanoids have a special emergency number. What is it? Five-five-five. No. Think, Oas! Think! Wait I know.

"Can someone call nine-one-one?" I begged.

Rotsen was still in my pocket. Either he'd fallen asleep or he didn't care that I was having a mental meltdown. Whichever it was, it wasn't how a friend was supposed to act. I know Lehcarr would have at least shown a little bit of concern for my predicament.

"Nic your friend is sure funny. Who calls nine-eleven for a brain freeze?" he asked.

I glanced up and noticed he was licking my ice cream. Funny, I didn't mind. If it had been Ralb, I would have thrown a major fit once my head stopped aching.

"She's just joking. How you feeling, April?" She reached out to rub my shoulder, much in the way my Parental Being did once.

I groaned and just as I feared I would have to live with this pain my entire time on your stupid planet, it stopped. Then nothing. It was as though it had never happened. I felt fine.

"It's gone," I admitted, looking at the two of them as they grinned and nodded.

"Anytime you eat something really cold, really fast, you'll get a brain freeze," the mawl explained.

Oh, no. Were these crazy humanoids going to

take my brain out and unfreeze it? I had gotten attached to it. I didn't want to have them remove it. Great! I glanced over toward the door. If I caught them off guard, I could make a run for it and probably find my way back to the lake. Ralb would just have to find his own way home.

Oops, I needed him to get back to Zorca-twenty-three.

"Calm down, April." Nicola put a mandible on me, and it instantly relaxed me. She was my friend. She wouldn't hurt me. Good thing Suzz wasn't here. She would have ripped out my brain and then eaten the rest of my ice cream without giving it a second thought.

"I've never experienced anything so painful before," I admitted. Nicola smiled at me, and even the mawl reached out and flicked my hair.

A warm jolt filled my insides instantly taking away the coldness of the ice cream. He was magic.

"Here's your ice cream back. Just eat it slowly. I'm Josh, by the way. Since Nic doesn't think I'm important enough to get introduced to you."

"Excuse me, Mr. Manners. April Oas, Josh Grant. Josh, April. April, he's a friend of my brother's and very annoying." Nicola licked at the cone shape, lapping her ice cream really fast because it was dripping.

What would happen if I ate this on Zorca-twenty-three, where there's zero gravity?

He punched Nicola in the arm. "I'm not maddening, like other people I could mention. You're the one who took Zac's iPod and hid it on him."

"It served him right. If he hadn't been teasing me about Owen, I wouldn't have bothered with it at all," Nicola said. "Do you know what it's like to have a brother who's a pain in the butt?"

Rotsen was rummaging through my pocket. I guess old sleepyhead was awake now. I had to bite my tongue because I opened my mouth to say, "Welcome to my world. See how you'd feel about having two hundred and fifty of them," but luckily I didn't.

"Owen is a friend of mine. He doesn't know it, but Nicola has a great big huge crush on him," Josh teased. "Anyway, are you guys leaving soon? I'll walk with you. I've got to see Zac to find out the schedule for tonight."

"I so do not. You are such a liar." She punched him in the arm. It must have hurt, because he rubbed it really hard. Then she turned toward me. "Are you okay now? Here, Josh, make yourself useful and hold my cone. And no eating it. I have to hit the can. April, give Josh your ice cream and come with me."

She took the paper bag with her new shirt and without another word, she grabbed my arm and pulled me along a small hallway. I almost tripped over her feet as I turned to take another gander at Josh, but I did as I was told. I had no idea how to hit the can. I was really regretting not studying for my trip.

She pushed open a door with the picture of an ice cream cone with a skirt on and pulled me through.

I stopped in shock.

Before me stood another Nicola, with a strange looking girl standing beside her. I reached out my mandible to touch the girl, but it bumped into a piece of glass. This glass wasn't see-through. It must have had stuff on the back of it because all I saw were two girls. It was like the looking glass at the clothing store.

Stars! It was me! I'd forgotten what I'd looked like when I left the salon. I appeared to be pretty. Heck, I wasn't just pretty. I was magazine pretty. I could be the cover on one of those glossy pages.

Our black hole needed some major updating.

I stood back and got a really good look at myself. I looked normal for a teenage girl. Considering I'd traveled at warp speed today and threw up a couple of times, I gave the impression of someone who'd just stepped off a fashion runway.

That Josh mawl was right. My hair was the same as Nicola's. Where hers was a waterfall, mine was more of a river, but you know what, despite everything it looked okay. The indoor sun in the salon didn't make it appear as bright as it did now. It almost seemed to be on fire, it was so bright and shiny.

My two eyes were perfectly placed on either side of a large protruding bone and I had an opening, I think they call it a mouth, right underneath it.

"You look like you've never seen yourself in a mirror before. Don't you remember being at Damon's and the clothing store? Must have been quite the brain freeze." Nicola looked over at me. She took a small thin tube out of her magic pocket and then pulled the top off it. She twisted up the end and whipped it around her lips, turning them bright pink. "Want to try it? We have about the same coloring. Josh is right. We could be cousins."

Almost trance-like I took the container from her and did as she had done. It felt like a layer of sheen now covered my opening. I remember seeing a girl on MTV wearing that color. I thought the movie people just naturally looked good.

"Thank you again for buying me a shirt," she said, opening the bag and hauling out the thin blue piece of material. "I think I'm going to change now."

She squished her lips together really tight and pulled her old shirt off, before sliding the new one on. She reached around, ripped the tags out of the neck and spun in front of the mirror.

"Well, what do you think?" She ran the tube of

sheen across her lips again. "I think you put Suzz's nose a little out of joint."

"I didn't touch her," I protested. I set the bag with my old clothes on the black counter and leaned against it.

"You are so funny. No, really, I think she's like jealous of you. Even if she is my BFF, you just have to be careful of her. Where did you get the outfit you were wearing earlier? It was so cool and original." Nicola's voice dropped to a whisper, and she walked over and with her foot pushed open each of the doors in the room. "Good we're all alone. Now, I don't know how much experience you've had with boys, but Josh likes you—a lot."

My head was buzzing with all the information. I'd almost forgotten she'd asked a question in there. What was I supposed to tell her about the outfit I'd arrived in? Could I just say I got it in my local black hole while jetting through space?

"So you're not going to tell me?" she asked.

I think she was miffed. I had to think of something—fast. Stick to the truth as much as you can. "I got it at The Black Hole."

"Great! When my parents get back from holidays can you take me?" She put her hands together and looked like Forzon, my long lost relative before he went to pieces.

See what happens when I don't think things through. Rotsen shook with laughter in my pocket. Now how was I going to get out of this? My only option was to get Ralb and get the heck home. But I didn't say that. "Of course I'll take you. I just have to remember where it is. I went to so many stores in one day trying to find the perfect outfit, so it's kind of a blur."

"Wow, that's great your mom takes you places. My mom and dad are so busy traveling or working, they never have time for my brother or me," she said as she washed her hands in the sink, then pushed a button on the wall and—whoosh—a vacuum dried her hands. Another note to add to my mist book. Driers of any type, first in the salon and now here, obsess planet Earth.

"Ummm, well, my mom doesn't take me places either. I was just trying to get her mind off my missing brother," I stammered, plus when you have so many offspring, the clothing allowance from the government doesn't really stretch too far.

"Are you guys going to be all day?" Josh called from the other side of the door.

"Hold your horses." Nicola rolled her eyes, a trick I was definitely going to have to learn. It looked so cool. "Come on. We'd better go. Don't worry, you look fine," she said to me as I glanced again at the mirror.

"If you say so," I said unsure of myself. I was a teenage alien with major anxiety issues. Maybe I would fit right in. But more importantly, where the heck did Josh get horses? I was about to ask when she interrupted my caboose of thoughts.

"Are you kidding me? I've already told you Josh has the hots for you."

I didn't know if that was good or bad, but after being cold in here and getting the frozen brain, I was glad someone was going to warm me up.

I walked through the brown door, which Nicola held open for me, straight into Josh, who looked embarrassed.

"Josh Grant, were you listening at the door?" Nicola asked in a voice that sounded like she already knew the answer to her question.

"Of course not. Let's go! Here's your ice cream, April." He gave it to me and licked Nicola's melted ice cream off his other hand. As he went to give Nicola her cone back, she moved at the same time and got a bit on her new blue top.

Her mom was going to be upset with all the laundry. I know my mom wouldn't be too chipper if I dirtied two outfits in less than an hour.

"What happened to my ice cream? It's half gone." I asked confused that it had evaporated so soon. That wasn't fair, Nicola's was still full sized, but dripping.

"I had to eat it. You guys took so long, it was melting." Josh smiled at me. He had two little dents, sort of cute little valleys on either side of his mouth, and when he smiled, they appeared. He was so hunky. Gorget could learn a thing or two about being nice to people. I was willing to bet the last dollar Rotsen handed me that he wouldn't be bossy either.

Josh Grant was better than any tree, bush, or shrub. Heck, he was even better looking than any celebrity I'd ever seen walk on the red carpet. I kid you not. He was a major Adonis on any planet in any solar system, including Pluto, which you guys don't think is a planet any longer.

"How come Nicola's is still the same?"

"I wouldn't eat hers. I didn't want to get cooties." Josh trailed his finger along my arm. The path he left was warm and tingly.

Nicola stopped licking her ice cream to stick her tongue out at him. I had so much to learn from this girl. She must be the Zen of Planet Earth.

After nodding to the group of mawls in the corner, Josh pulled open the outside door and walked through. Then he held it open for Nicola and me. We strolled along the white cement strip with me in the middle and my two new friends on either side.

"Do you live far from here?" I asked after I finished my ice cream. It didn't take long since it was already mostly eaten.

"Just over on Elm Street. Josh lives on Maple Avenue. Suzz is over on the rich side of town on a farm called CastleRock," Nicola said, between licks.

"You're so lucky having your best friend live so close to you. Mine lives on another planet." Oh, stars, what did I just say? Why is it as a humanoid I can't control my mouth?

"You're right, Nic, she is really funny and cute, too," Josh said.

He looked sideways at me, and I got really warm. Maybe that's what Nicola meant when she said Josh had the hots for me. He did make me warm. Funny how I could feel heated, though, when my skin looked like a chicken's, all covered in small bumps.

He stopped in the middle of the cement and turned me around to face him. He reached forward and touched my nose. So I did what any ananoid would do, I slapped him. Not nearly as effective as it was when I used my antenna, but it had the same result.

Oops, I don't think I was supposed to do that. I might have put his nose out of joint.

"What the snap was that for? I was just wiping a bit of ice cream off your nose. Man, you pack a wallop." He bent over with his head in his hands, and his ball cap fell to the ground.

I bent down to pick it up, figuring it was the least I could do, and realized I'd made another mistake. I had on very tight, low-riding jeans, so when I went to grab his cap for him, I think he could see my exposed back skin. He definitely could see my inner coverings. I hoped I was wearing something pretty. To be honest, when I'd changed at the jean store, I'd been more impressed with the orbs in the front of my shirt to notice anything about what was on the bottom.

Everything must have been okay, because when I handed him back his hat, he grinned. Again he made me hot. I guess I wouldn't need a jacket on

Earth after all.

"Are you two just about done? Why don't you get a room somewhere?" Nicola said, now that her cone was finished.

"You're right, Nicola," I said, totally agreeing with her. She had put into words what I'd been thinking not too long ago.

"What?" Josh said in a hopeful tone. "You want to get a room?"

I knew I was missing something when a mawl was getting worked up and excited about where I was going to lay my head and nod off. I'd studied enough to remember I wasn't supposed to hang upside down in a cave somewhere. "Well, I have to sleep somewhere tonight."

"Oh," Josh said, sounding sad. He kicked hard at a white stone, and it bounced out on the black tar path.

"Don't worry about a thing. You can stay at my house. My parents are away, and it's only my brother and me at home. I have a big lock on my bedroom door to keep Josh out," Nicola said, elbowing him in the ribs.

"I don't know how to thank you. For the room I mean." I linked arms with Nicola. It made me really happy to be intertwined with her.

"Great! Thanks, Nicola. I don't know how to thank you either," Josh said. I don't think he really wanted to thank her at all. In fact, if I didn't know better, I'd say he was a little ticked off.

"Good! That's all settled then," Nicola confirmed. "Josh, I just remembered. Zac is working at Pizza Party this afternoon. He took the early shift so he could be off tonight. He wanted me to tell you to go there at five forty-five and help him carry home the pizzas. You're supposed to phone him to confirm."

I cringed after the word pizza and blocked out the rest.

"Sure!" I watched him feel around in his pockets for something. His shorts had a lot more room than Nicola's jeans, but then again they also hung down to his ankles. "Snap! I left my cell at home. I'll run home, phone him and then come back with him to your house."

"Okay," Nicola said. "Whatever."

"I'll see you later, April." Josh rubbed my shoulder in a really nice way before he left us.

"Bye," I said back. I looked over my shoulder and saw he'd stopped in the middle of the street and stood watching us walk away. He was so nice. He didn't want us to get lost. But I hoped he was careful. Josh better watch out for those four-wheeled dragonflies. They were dangerous.

"Come on, April. We have a lot to do to get ready for tonight." Nicola pulled up the sleeve of her blue shirt and peered down at a small circular device that appeared to be ticking. I wondered if she realized she had a bomb attached to her arm. But I decided she was a smart girl, so it didn't just end up there without her knowing.

Nicola tugged at my arm. "First I have to stop at Olivia's house."

"Why?" I asked. After stumbling three times, I turned away from Josh and watched where I was walking.

"I have to look after her while her mom runs to the grocery store. I do it every Saturday at this time." Together we raced up the street as fast as our tight jeans would allow and then stopped in front of a building higher than any I'd ever seen before.

"She lives on the top floor of this apartment building." Nicola pushed a series of buttons and, with buzzers and ringers, the door opened and we walked through. "Want to take the elevator or the stairs?"

Not knowing what the first thing she'd

mentioned was, I played it safe and said the stairs.

"Okay, if you're game, I am too. It probably wouldn't hurt to have a bit of exercise between now and the partee. Especially when I plan on eating some of my brother's famous pizza," Nicola said as she pushed open a metal door.

"Oh, this won't be so bad." Behind the door was a set of steps. I counted fifteen in all, then the upside-down steps.

Nicola gave me a strange look, but I was too excited to get stairing.

I trotted up the first set of stairs like I was a marathon runner. I'd seen the Boston Marathon race, and I was running faster than they did.

I completed the first set. When I got to the landing, I stopped, confused. Leaning over to catch my breath, I asked. "Where's the apartment?"

"Oh, there are still lots more steps to go." Nicola grinned. "Come on, lazybones. It'll do you good."

Good? Right! It would kill me. I would be joining Forzon a heck of a lot faster than I'd planned. My air sacs must have been ill equipped for the climb because after only ten flights, I was ready to sit down on the cement.

"Do I have to remind you, you were the one who wanted to take the stairs?" Nicola leaned on the railing and grinned down at me.

"I didn't know there were going to be so many." I panted and worried my breath would never return to its normal state.

"What did you expect? Olivia lives on the top floor." Nicola's breath was normal. She was even running in the exact same place.

"H-how m-many more?" I tried to inhale like I did before I started this climb up the highest cement mountain on Earth.

She glanced over at the door with a number one and zero on it.

"We're almost there. Just three more." She grabbed my hand to pull me up, but I only succeeded in pulling her down with me.

"Three more steps?" I begged. "Please tell me you meant only three more steps."

"Oh, come on, you silly goose. Let's get moving. The sooner we get there, the sooner we can leave and get ready for the partee."

"Are you kidding me? Partee! After this, I'm going to go to the bed you offered me and sleep until there are three moons in the sky." I let her pull me up this time. Leaning heavily on the railing beside the steps, I dragged myself upward. To keep my mind off the aches that were bombarding my body, I read the writing on the wall.

Painted with bright orange paint, LL hearted GG, and if you ever wanted a good time, you were to call Suzz. To be honest, this surprised me. If it was the same Suzz I knew, she didn't look like a fun person. I didn't know how she could add some more excitement to any occasion. But, hey, what did I know? She might have many hidden talents I knew nothing about.

When we reached the top, it was a miracle, which says a lot coming from someone who space traveled today. An optical illusion awaited us, but when I blinked my eyes again, I realized it was the door we sought. Next time we were definitely taking the easy way. With more energy than I could have mustered, Nicola grasped the door handle and yanked.

Nothing.

"Oh, guess what?" she asked when I finally reached her side. "The door's locked."

The look that crossed my face made her burst out laughing.

"I'm only joshing you. Come on, let's go and see Olivia." She linked her arm with mine—probably she needed the support from the climb—and knocked on the door on the left of the hallway.

A scream emanated from inside, which caused her to laugh.

"April, you're really going to like Olivia. She's a real card." Nicola stood at one side of the door, so when the girl opened the door, she was hidden. The girl was about four Earth years old and had hair the color of the black tar paths. She wore a matching purple sweatshirt and pants and little purple socks. Seeing only me, she burst into tears.

"Boo," Nicola yelled.

The little femawl's tears dried up. She rushed toward Nicola and threw her mandibles around my friend's walking sticks. I would have been knocked down, but Nicola only laughed.

The little humanoid wiped a drippy nose on Nicola's jeans, then tilted her head back and smiled.

"Hi, baby girl." Nicola ran her fingers though the femawl's hair.

"I'm not a baby girl." She pouted. "Besides, what took you so long to get upstairs?"

"My friend and I decided to walk it." Nicola smiled toward me.

"It's a lot of steps," Olivia said.

"Tell me about it," I said, still exhausted.

"I thought I heard voices out here." An older version of Olivia entered the room. She wiped her hands on a towel and then flung it over her shoulder. "Pardon the mess," she directed her words in my direction. "Olivia has been feeling under the weather, so I've been on entertainment committee all day long. I haven't had time to clean up."

"You sound like my mom." I had a slight twinge of Zorca-twenty-three sickness. "She always says our cave is a pig sty, and we don't even have pigs."

"That is so familiar. My mom says my room is too messy for pigs to even want to stay in." She laughed. "They're the cleanest animals in the barnyard."

"So I guess my mom doesn't want me to clean up then." I smiled.

"Thanks for coming today, Nicola. I just need to run out and get some basics. Milk, bread, you know."

"And don't forget ice cream. You promised ice cream." Olivia squealed as Nicola tickled her.

"Just watch out for the brain freeze," I warned. I was now a humanoid expert on brain-frozen objects.

"Only babies get brain freezes," Olivia said with confidence, which caused Nicola to laugh.

"Mrs. Ashbridge, this is my friend April. Is it okay if she stays?"

Olivia pulled Nicola down onto the sofa. The little girl grabbed a picture book and crawled into Nicola's lap.

"Please say yes." I sank down onto the other sofa. "I don't think I could handle all those stairs again. In fact, I might have to move in here."

Everyone, including Olivia, laughed, which confused me. They thought I was joking. Little did they know I was very serious.

"Of course, she can stay." Mrs. Ashbridge grabbed a *hanaglug* and opened it. I expected a Rotsen to pop out, but nothing did. She added some Earth paper money from a candy jar on the counter and turned to face her daughter. "Olivia. I think Nicola's friend needs some water. Why don't you get her a glass from the kitchen?"

The little girl scurried off.

Her Parental Being—oh, right, on Earth they're called moms—her mom came over and stood close to Nicola. I used the opportunity to investigate the square room with my newfound eyes.

Every available surface was covered with copies of Olivia. Her face was surrounded by pieces of wood and attached to the wall. There were shelves beside a humongous pile of stones against the wall and even they were loaded down with faces of Olivia.

Stars above, I don't think Oscar people had that many pictures taken of them, and they were celebrities. But then maybe Olivia was, too.

How awesome was that! I was in the home of a real famous person. My sticks twitched in excitement, and I covered my eating hole—oh right, mouth—with my hand. Nicola and Mrs. Ashbridge both peered over at me with the hair above their eyes raised, but I didn't care what they thought.

I was so going to get Olivia's signature.

Stars, I wished I'd brought some kind of writing instrument.

Olivia came back into the room with a glass full of liquid and handed it to me.

"Thank you," I said as I took it from her. "Olivia, would you happen to have something to write with?"

"Sure, I've got lots of markers." She held out her hand, and we walked together down a long, thin room to another room. The water in the glass wouldn't stay in place and kept swishing around.

In the distance I heard a door shut, but I wasn't interested. Instead I entered the little girl's sleeping quarters, and my jaw dropped open. I lifted my hand to put it back in its proper position, but it did it again, so I just left it where it was.

Trancelike I entered and put the glass down on the closest surface. I didn't want to spill anything in this famous person's home.

What caused my shock were the decorations. I could now understand why the other area had been filled with faces of Olivia. I took a moment to pat myself on the back of my body, not the easiest thing to do, but I managed, even if I did get a sore neck. That's what humanoids did to congratulate themselves, so I was due for some major backslapping.

The girl was a princess.

Obviously.

There was a large, flat bed centered in the middle with four sticks reaching up to a piece of material draped across the top.

But what caught my two eyes more than anything were the golden crowns. They were everywhere.

Like a magnet, they pulled me closer. I had to touch one, feel a real one.

Olivia bounded in ahead of me and jumped on her bed, her actions causing the crowns to shift on the table, the jewels on the closest one catching the light from outside and sparkling.

"May I touch it?" I asked Olivia, who had finished bouncing and now lay down.

The bouncing had taken a lot out of her, because it was all she could do to lift her hand up and give it to me.

"It's called a tiara and it goes on your head." She snuggled down on the bed, reminding me for a minute of Forzon and how he'd acted the same way in my hand, just before I'd squished him.

She placed the tiara on my head and turned me toward a reflecting piece of wall.

Wow, I was now a princess, just like in the movies.

"Nicola's friend," Olivia said as she tugged at my arm. "I'm really thirsty. Can I have some of your water?"

"Of course." I handed it to her and helped while she had a big gulp. I placed it back on the table, and she snuggled down under the princess coverings.

"I'm going to have a little sleep now." She drew a fluffy white dog closer to her tiny body. "Maybe when I wake up, we can have a tea party."

"Sure." I glanced back over at her small body in the big bed and smiled down at her.

"Okay, are we ready to partee?" Nicola shouted, pumping her hands in the air as she came into the princess area.

"Is the mother back already?" I removed the tiara, put it back on the table, and patted it once for goodbye.

"No, I meant the three of us. When I come to babysit, we always have a dress-up party." She glanced over at Olivia's sleeping form. "How unusual. Her mom told me she wasn't feeling up to par." She grabbed my arm and pulled me out of the room. "Come on. I want to know all about you."

Oh, great!

She sat at one end of the surprisingly soft sofa and I, at the other. I'd learned from my *wad* what they were called. Stars above, there sure are a lot of advertisements to sell them on your television.

"You know what, Nicola." I had to think fast and, unfortunately, that wasn't my area of expertise. "I'd rather know about you."

"Okay, I'll go first." She shifted on the sofa and tucked her long sticks under her body. I tried to copy her move, but only ended up kicking my one leg with the other.

She burst out laughing and slapped me on the shoulder. "You just slay me." She threw a blanket over our sticks before she continued. "There's not much to tell. I grew up in this town. My parents travel a lot. Zac is my brother, and he's a major pain in the butt most times, but then sometimes he can be really nice." She smiled. "Okay, your turn."

Stars! What was I going to say? Rotsen shifted in my pocket, no doubt laughing at the predicament I'd gotten myself into.

"There's not much to tell." I started the same way she did. "I'm looking for my brother because my mom wants him at home. I couldn't care less if I ever saw him again. I mean when you have over five hundred siblings, what's one less?"

Stars, did I just say that?"

"See that's what I mean. You are just so funny. So if you could go on a dream date with anyone, where would you go and with who?" She asked, picking at the small shells on the ends of her hands. "For me, it would be Orlando Bloom and a deserted island."

"Oh, this one is easy for me." I shivered at the thought. "Definitely Johnny Depp, and it could be anywhere and anytime."

"Well, at least we're not fighting over the same guy." Nicola laughed. She rotated her eyes to a moving circle on the wall. "Mrs. Ashbridge should be home anytime. Then we'll leave and walk back to my place."

"You don't look after Olivia very long. When I have to babysit all my brothers, my Parental Being, I mean my mom, is gone for days." I copied Nicola's movements. She was using her second finger to pick skin off her thumb.

"Probably because you have so many."

She laughed and I smiled.

She picked up a small rectangular box from the table and, after she pushed some buttons, the television clicked on. With her finger pressed on the red one, the television shows rotated.

Finally, she stopped on one, and we watched a show about the problems on Earth.

"I hate it when there's nothing on the boob tube." She settled back onto the sofa and began flipping though a shiny magazine with a pretty woman on the cover.

I leaned forward, so intent on the contents of the show that I had to grab the edge of the table in front of me. I'd forgotten my sticks were tucked under me. I pushed myself back and listened to a man with a funny accent.

"A small town in Ontario, Canada, has had a recent outbreak of E.coli poisoning in the water. The flu-like symptoms have affected the majority of the townspeople, even resulting in some deaths. Stay tuned for further developments."

"Nicola?" I tried to get her attention. I glanced over to see what she was reading, and she appeared to be involved in an article about how to win friends. I could save her the time. Everyone knows to win anything on any planet, you have go to the Internet auctions and outbid every other humanoid in the solar system.

"Umm."

"Do you know what E. coli is?" I continued watching the television, in the hopes of learning more, but it switched to the weather report.

"No. What do you think of this sweater?" She asked, holding the magazine up for me to see. "I can't imagine why anyone would wear a black sweater with a green skirt. You have to admit that combo is hideous."

Before I could reply, there was a sound at the door, and Mrs. Ashbridge opened it, her hands filled with paper bags.

Nicola jumped off the sofa and went to grab them and carry them into another area of the apartment.

"Was Olivia good?" She asked as she took off her coat and hung her purse on a stick rod.

"You're right about her feeling under the weather. She fell asleep almost as soon as you left, and she's been out like a light ever since." Nicola answered, as she came back in.

Mrs. Ashbridge approached and handed her a wad of paper money, which Nicola pocketed. The woman tried to give me some, but I shook my head. I had plenty of money and only a limited time to spend it.

"Thank you, and I'll see you the same time next week," she said to Nicola. Then she smiled at me. "Thanks again for your help. It was nice to meet you."

Nicola pulled open the door, and we were in the hall, facing an enormous amount of stairs once again.

"You're not going to make me go back down all of them again, are you?" I asked, almost vomiting at the thought. Cripes, if I threw up anymore today, I'd definitely be considered anorexic.

"We can take the elevator."

"Thank you." I followed her down to the end of the hallway where there was one button on the wall beside a metal door. She pushed it and, after we waited a bit, the door creaked open, revealing a small hidden room.

It was very tiny. There was a small crack between the hallway floor and the bottom of the box. When I peered downward, I could see lights through the crevice. The multi-tiered cave was falling apart.

I screamed.

"Just jump," Nicola said with the patient tone I'd heard her use with Olivia.

Easy for her to say. I backed up against the hall and took a long run into the little box. I smashed my face against the back wall, but I was inside. For better or for worse, I was inside the brightly lit cave with Nicola.

I couldn't breathe. I couldn't catch my breath. I grasped the metal bars lining the inside and hung on for dear life.

Nicola pushed one of the round buttons on the wall, and the doors creaked into operation. The humanoid eating-machine rushed to close us up inside.

"Wait," I screamed.

But we plummeted towards the inner sanctum

of Earth. Down, down, down we went at the speed of light or just about.

I opened my mouth to tell her I was going to get out and walk. My ears popped, and then a miracle occurred.

The doors slid open, and I saw daylight.

We were facing a large room filled with foresty plants and chairs that didn't look used. Sunlight trickled in through the wall's high glass.

I'd survived.

I pumped my fist in the air and locked arms with Nicola. Together we strolled outside. I swung my bag with my old clothes in it like I didn't have a care in the world. I didn't. I'd traveled through black holes, survived a hairdresser, eaten ice cream, done an endurance walk up countless steps, and finally lived to tell about my adventure in an elevator.

No wonder I was feeling a tad asteroid-lagged.

My mouth released a yawn, and Nicola grinned.

"Girlfriend, we have a lot to do before all the guests arrive." Nicola smoothed down her hair and twisted it back into a tail without the use of anything other than another piece of hair.

"So you're still having that partee?" I would have thought we'd had enough excitement for the day.

"Of course. It's a tradition. When the parents are away, the kids partee," Nicola said. "Owen promised to come. I want to show you a picture of him, so you can stay away from him. I don't want any competition from you. He promised me he was going to give me a night to remember."

"I wouldn't like someone you like. It wouldn't be right," I said to my Earth BFF. "Who would do something so mean?"

"Not mentioning any names, but it's a good thing Suzz hates Josh, because she'd try and wreck things for you. I love her to death, but I wouldn't trust her as far as I could throw her."

"But sometime in the near future, I have to find my brother." I didn't really want to, but figured I should protest a little bit. After all whether I liked it or not, Ralb was the reason I was here, the reason I'd met Josh, and I did feel a little remorse. How would my mom feel if I went back to Zorca-twenty-three without him?

"If your brother is anywhere in a fifty-mile radius, he'll be here. My brother Zac has been planning this partee for weeks."

"So my brother will come here?" I wanted to see him, of course, but hoped he wouldn't ruin anything I might have going with Josh.

"April, there will be so many boys here, you'll be able to have your pick of brothers." Nicola linked her arm through mine again. "I think I'll wash the ice cream off this shirt and wear it tonight. Suzz will be so mad. She's had her eye on it for weeks."

I opened my mouth to say, I already had more than enough brothers, when Rotsen wriggled in my pocket. I'd have to let him loose soon, or I'd never hear the end of it. Besides you don't want to tick off a fan of *The Sopranos*. He might get me whacked.

I was going to my first Earth partee. If there was pizza there, I was so going to try it. Zen said it wouldn't cause me any problems, unlike popcorn. Heck, I might even attempt eating popcorn as well. I'd survived traveling through a drop in a small machine, how could a little corn of pop hurt me? Speaking of pop, I was dying—well, not really—but I did want to try one of the one hundred and sixty-three varieties of pop this town is known for.

Oh, yeah, I also must find Ralb.

Well, first things first.

## Chapter Ten

We walked past houses with lots of short green leafy spikes all over the front yards and plants with flowers in just about every color of the rainbow. I had to stop myself from throwing myself down on the plots of green grass. I prevented myself from taking the flowers and smelling them. I knew they'd make me sneeze. Each of the houses had a flag identical to one of the ones I saw on the Space Station. I glanced around for one of the red and white ones with a maple leaf, but I guess they were all out.

Nicola gave me a running commentary of what was going on behind each of the front doors. *Desperate Housewives* had nothing on this street. I only halfheartedly listened, as I was more interested in the foliage and fauna abounding around the houses. The trees were all bushy and lush in their different shades of greenness. It surprised me humanoids could have their very own plantations.

I couldn't help myself, I ran up to a deep purple flower, which looked like a hanging upside down ice cream cone. I inhaled the fragrance. My nose tickled. My face took on a life of its own as it ordered my eyes to squeeze shut. A loud honking noise erupted from my nose. That was bad enough, but tiny drops of water sprayed out of my nose.

"Bless you," Nicola said to me, for some strange reason.

"Bless you too, sisterhood." I answered back.

"You say *bless you* or *gesundheit* when someone sneezes. It's German for *God bless you.*" She peered at me as if I was an alien, which of course I was. "You act like you've never heard of those sayings before."

Thank stars, she didn't wait for an answer, but just shrugged her shoulders.

"Did you know when you sneeze you stop breathing?" Nicola added.

Great! Now not only did I have to worry about popcorn and pizza, but if I smelled anything odd and sneezed, I'd quit breathing. I'm pretty darn sure that wasn't mentioned in the mist book.

"See the house there, with the shutters." She pointed to a dwelling with cocoa-brown wooden slats attached to each of the windows. "I used to babysit their youngest, a little girl named Heidi."

"Did you get fired?"

"No, she died. She was only six years old. I went to her funeral last week. It was so sad. You should have seen the casket." I looked over at her and saw her eyes peeing.

I didn't think it was the time to ask what a casket was, but it was obviously something that made you sad. I stopped walking and on instinct wrapped my mandibles around her small torso.

"Thanks, April. I needed a hug." She used her hands to wipe her watery eyes, and we continued walking.

"See that house there?"

It reminded me of my cave as it only had one row of glass windows. Painted a bright yellow color that rivaled Rotsen's petals, even its flag hung silent. "Mrs. Walker lived there, but she died two weeks ago."

I stopped, prepared to hug her again, but there wasn't any water sprouting from her eyes. "Was she not in a casket? Is that why you're not sad?"

"Oh, no, she was in a casket. But she was old," Nicola said, as if it explained everything.

Stars, these humanoids were hard to figure out. If you were young in a casket it was a bad thing, old in a casket, then everything was a-okay. Though from the sounds of all this dying going on in this town, Forzon would have a lot of company.

She turned and walked onto a black driveway. "Where are we going now? Did someone die here, too?"

"I hope not. It's my house," Nicola said, with a slight smile, "though if Mom and Dad find out about the partee, there might be a death here."

From the look on my face she realized I didn't think she was joking. "It's okay, really. I was trying to be funny, but I'm not a natural comedian like you are."

"You live here? It's a mansion." I stood in amazement. I couldn't believe I knew someone who actually lived in one of these abodes.

Her house looked like a castle. It was made from big, odd-shaped stones with a rounded room at the front that went all the way to the roof. There was a covering over the doorway. It went right along the side of the house. Someone had put two chairs there and in between them was a table, which held a big container, filled with red, pink, and white flowers. They kind of smelled funny even from back where I stood, but they sure looked pretty.

"Come on in," Nicola called to me. She opened a door with wire all over it, pushed down on a metal knob, and voilà, the door sprang backwards.

"Don't you have a key?" I asked, because on the satellite, Earthlings locked up everything whether it was valuable or not. I don't think she'd want anyone to steal her house.

"April, this is Bedrocktown. Nothing ever happens here." She sighed. "We don't even have a crime section in our newspaper."

I briefly thought about all the caskets being

used, but didn't want to bring it up in case she started again with the waterworks.

I followed her lead, hoping she was going to give me a map, because I didn't think I'd be able to find my way to the front door again. I passed rooms that didn't look like they'd ever been used. Obviously, she didn't have as many brothers as I did.

We stopped in a room I'd never seen before. It was filled with machines humming and clicking, and it was really warm. I was hot just standing in there. Not as hot as Josh made me feel, but pretty close.

"We'll get a bite in a sec. Oh, I could strangle Zac. He took his own stuff out of the dryer and left some of mine in a heap on the floor. The rest he left inside. Great. Now, I'm going to have to iron. I hate it."

"Me, too!" I had no idea what ironing was, but it sounded like something involving work.

"Okay, now that's done." She pulled open the door of a big square machine, and then her hands and arms disappeared inside. They came out holding a black shirt and blue jeans, which she hung on two separate hangers. Seemed to me it was easier to shop in the black hole, even if you did end up with a tremendous headache for your troubles.

"Are you hungry?" Nicola asked as I followed her into another room with large machines. These were shiny and metal. They reminded me of miniature space ships, but for some reason I didn't think they flew anywhere.

"Not really, more tired than anything," I admitted. The space traveling was catching up to me. I had a major case of asteroid lag.

"I guess you're pretty stressed trying to find your brother. Why don't you go upstairs to the second room on the right and have a nap? That's our spare room. Feel free to use it for as long as you like," Nicola said.

I didn't want to appear difficult, so I followed her suggestion.

"Thanks, I think I will." I grabbed the plastic bag with my old clothes in it and headed toward the stairs. A groan and a moan escaped my mouth.

Stars above. What is it with this stupid planet and steps? When I put my foot on the first step, my body protested.

"How many are there?" I had a hard time getting the words out, as panic filled my very being.

"Just these. I promise." She had come to stand behind me. She laughed.

"I'm glad you think it's funny. I can barely move after all those steps at the apartment building." I grabbed the railing and with utmost determination used my arms to pull my poor aching body up each step.

I opened my mouth to say on my planet you didn't have to use stupid stairs, because you could fly everywhere. I was interrupted by a ringing sound. It stopped and then started again. Stopped and rang again.

"I'll grab the phone. You head up for your rest." Nicola picked up a sausage-shaped piece of metal and spoke into it. Covering the bottom part of the phone she said to me, "It's Suzz. I'll tell her you said hi."

I nodded and began the long climb upstairs. I counted off the doors, but I must have gotten the wrong door because I entered a mawl's room.

It didn't look like a spare room. There didn't look like there was anything spare about it at all. In fact there was no room for a spare.

There were sports items for all the Earthling games I'd ever seen or read about. Soccer balls lined up alongside footballs. Jerseys in every color imaginable hung from every surface. They were hanging on hooks inserted into the ceiling. Metal rods protruded from the walls to hold hockey sticks and helmets.

I was getting a real humanoid lesson here and wasn't sure what to make of it. I'd always thought Earthlings slept on horizontal beds. But there was no room for the owner of this room to sleep in his bed. It was covered with socks, jeans, T-shirts, and sweatshirts.

I don't think they were clean. From the odor emanating from the room, something must have died in there. I'd have to tell Nicola, but first I had to retrace my steps and find my spare room.

I recounted the doors and found, thankfully, I had added wrong. Zen wouldn't be impressed that I couldn't even do a simple math problem in my brain. I opened the door to my room afraid of what I might find. I breathed a sigh of relief. This was like the one I saw in the Martha Stewart book on the Internet.

I walked in and sat down on the bed, which was covered in a flowered quilt and had a yellow blanket folded at the bottom and nothing else. There was nothing out of place, unlike Zac's room. Nicola's family must be really rich if they had so many rooms they had extras. The walls were painted a light brown color, reminding me of chocolate ice cream, which made my inner torso rumble. The white furniture had the same brown on its trim. There were window coverings Martha would be proud of, two on either side of the window in a light gauzy material.

After kicking off my shoes, I lay back on the bed and tried out the pillow under my head. It felt perfect. I reached down to the bottom of the bed and pulled the yellow blanket up.

Even Rotsen flipping around couldn't disturb me. I was out like a light bulb. I slept the sleep of the dead, and I didn't even need a casket. Good thing. I didn't want Nicola to start peeing out her eyes.

Chapter Eleven

"April, are you going to get up?" The bed vibrated and shook. It wouldn't stop. I rolled over and groaned. Slowly I opened one of my two eyes and found Nicola now dressed in the jeans from the dryer and the shirt I'd purchased for her.

"You look nice," I said, stretching like a cat. "How long did I sleep?"

"About two hours. I tried to be quiet, but come on if you want to have a shower before my brother gets home. Believe me, you don't want to get in there after him. Major revoltingness." She grabbed my hand and pulled me off the bed. "Our other bathroom had a major water leak from the shower, so my dad said it was off-limits until it's fixed. Talk about having to rough it."

"Okay, okay, I'm up. Point me in the direction, and I'll go and have one of these showers." I stumbled towards the door, then turned and ran back to the bed. I tried to rearrange the coverings the way they'd been when I came in. I hoped I'd get to use this bed again.

Nicola waited for me at the door. "Hello? My mom's not home. It doesn't really matter if the bed's made or not."

"It matters to me. Sorry it's as good as I can get it." I went to the door, and she pointed to another doorway. I felt like I was on a game show, unsure what was going to appear behind door number four.

I entered and found a Mecca of porcelain. There was a hole in the counter with a bowl underneath it, a small lake in the middle of another bowl. This one sat on the floor and then a tiled room with glass doors.

"Here's a towel for you." Nicola reached under the counter and pulled out a fluffy blue sheet, which looked like it was large enough to fit on the bed. "I'll start the taps for you because it's kind of tricky. My dad is an okay guy, but he's not a plumber. He mixed up the hot and cold water taps, so get out before you try to readjust them or you might get burned." I watched her slide open the doors and lean over the metal circle.

I jumped backwards when an indoor water fountain started.

"I'll leave you to it. Feel free to use the shampoo and soaps. Do you want to borrow fresh clothes?" she asked, eyeing my outfit. "Though I can understand if you want to keep on the ones you have. They are so cool."

"I'll see how I feel once I get out," I said, as I struggled to get out of the jeans and shirt, which seemed to be glued to my skin.

Nicola grinned at me and then left the room, closing the door as she went. As I finished taking my clothes off, I turned towards the mirror, the indoor waterfall momentarily forgotten.

I was in shock as to what my coverings had been, well, covering.

When I'd been at the store trying clothes on, I knew things were sticking out where they normally wouldn't, but I'd been too clothes-happy to study them. Now I had the time and the opportunity.

I had two melon-shaped bumps on the front of my chest, which wouldn't have looked out of place on Xron's tree pot.

I ran my hands down each of my sides, surprised at the curves. My abdomen was so flat, any celebrity would be proud to own it. And it was all mine, at least temporarily.

A loud knocking interrupted my investigating. The pounding was followed by a deep voice. "Hey, new friend of my annoying sister, can you get a move on? I've been working all day, and I need a shower."

"Sorry, I'll just be an eon, I mean a second." I jumped into the shower and stood under the downfall. It was heaven. All the tiredness and sleepiness seemed to head down the drain with the water.

I turned my back to the shower and poured some of Nicola's shampoo onto my hair, then lathered it in like I'd seen on commercials. I followed suit with all the bottles in there. Some smelled so good, I couldn't resist. I tilted my head backward, and the strawberry/kiwi flavors slid into my mouth. It might have smelled like a fruit salad, but it tasted like soap. Gagging, I leaned forward and spit out the suds. No wonder I never saw any of the famous people eating it. It smelt good, but tasted horrible.

I cupped the warm cascading water in my mandibles and sucked it up, which only made the matter worse. The water tasted horrid.

I spat it out.

Big time yuckiness.

I coughed and put my arms up in the air to get oxogyen into my air sacs. It worked. This planet was trying to kill me. First with the brain freeze, then with the water. Honestly, our water on Zorca-twenty-three wasn't the best in the galaxy, but the water here in Bedrocktown was downright horrible.

Ugh! I grabbed the end of the towel sheet and rubbed the inside of my mouth with it.

Again the pounding interrupted my shower, so I jumped out as she advised me to. I followed Nicola's instructions and bent over and twisted the knobs. I wasn't coordinated enough though. A burst of freezing water splattered on the back of my neck. When I finally figured out the correct way to turn them, the water drizzled to a trickle, then to nothing. Relieved, I grabbed the towel sheet Nicola had left for me. I wrapped it around myself and was enveloped in a cloud of softness. Almost like being surrounded by a caring mother's arms, not that I would know the feeling.

I gathered up my clothes and opened the door, letting the steam in the room escape into the hallway. I had my towel held up with one hand and my clothes in the other and ran smack dab into a mawl I hoped was Nicola's brother.

"Hi, I'm Zac. You must be April. I hope you left some hot water for me. I could have joined you, and we could have saved some water." He grinned to show me he was kidding, I think.

My face felt warm. I rushed into my spare room and shut the door. I looked for a lock, but there wasn't one.

Rotsen was furious. He twisted and turned in my pocket like a leaf blowing in the wind. I remorphed the piece of chalk, so it changed back into my *hanaglug*, and then I let the squirming and complaining *tootoo* out of his prison.

"You got some 'plaining to do! What are you thinking leaving me in there for so long? I could have suffocated. I could have died. Then you'd have my death on your hands. How would you have liked that? Not very much. I can tell you that right now. Wow, look at these digs. You scored big time here. Who'd you have to whack to get this room?" His voice ran on a mile a minute.

"Shhh! They're going to hear you. I didn't whack anybody. Now be quiet for a minute. I've got to look up something in the mist book." I reached deeper into the *hanaglug* and pulled out my traveling guide. I ignored Rotsen as I flipped frantically through the pages searching for an answer, the reason why the water was so revolting.

"I've been cooped up in a hunk of chalk for stars knows how long, and you want me to be quiet?" He twisted his stem around and sat on the back of the *hanaglug*, leaves crossed.

"I drank some of the water, which came out of their indoor water fountain, and it tasted ghastly. I need to find out why. Is there something wrong with me?"

"Zen arranged things for you so you'd be completely self-reliant on Earth. There's no reason at all this water should be affecting your system. You should have been able to digest it without any problem," he said in a know-it-all voice. I think he sensed my concern, because he'd dropped the fake Italian accent. I was getting my old Rotsen back, pure and simple.

"So tell me something I don't know?" I flipped open the book and waited impatiently as the pages toward the back of the book slowly took shape.

"April, are you coming?" Nicola's voice called from a great distance away.

"I'll be right there. Rotsen, I need a huge favor!" I dropped my towel and hurriedly put my clothes back on.

"Wooza, look at you. You look fantastic. You could get a job at the Bada Bing," Rotsen said after a high-pitched whistle.

I gave him a look to shut him up. "Okay, now listen, you pervert. I need you to read through this book and summarize the water chapter. It's important that I leave now. *Jobe* you piles."

"Sure, I bet you say those words to everyone you want a favor from." He pouted.

I leaned over and kissed him on his right petal. "Tuck yourself into the *hanaglug* when you're finished."

"Yes, boss. But I wanted to go to the party. I never get to have any fun. This trip isn't all about you, you know," he said, crossing his leaves and showing me major attitude.

"Shut up. I know that. Now do it—please." I checked myself out in the mirror that hung over the wooden box with six drawers. I fluffed my hair, pinched my cheeks like I'd seen the girls do on *Eight Simple Rules*, and waved good-bye to Rotsen.

"April," he said in a sarcastic tone, "don't forget to find your brother. Do you need a picture to remember what he looks like?"

"He's my brother. I think I'll know. Besides Zen made sure it was etched in my memory. He erased the Oscar shrine in my brain and replaced it with one of Bertie in different poses. That's why I have to find him. I want the red carpet back." I didn't want to tell him Josh might be replacing the golden statue in my fave department. If you thought teasing from a brother was bad, you've never encountered the barbed tongue of my Rotsen.

"Glad it's for such a selfless reason," Rotsen said as I shut the door on him.

134

Chapter Twelve

When I entered the kitchen, Josh, Zac, and Nicola were sitting around a high counter, glasses filled with liquids in front of each of them. There was a pile of five square boxes in the middle emitting an amazing aroma.

"Hi, April. Come and sit here. I saved you a spot." Josh slid over and patted an empty seat beside him.

"Thanks." I stood on my tippy toes and tried to get onto the stool. I wasn't tall enough, but bless his heart he put his arms around my waist and pulled me up. I was surprised when he kept his one arm there. In fact, he tucked his hand into the pocket on my bum. It wasn't an easy thing to do, because of my pants being so tight, but he managed. They must be expandable like Nicola's. How else could she get gum, lipstick, and everything else in them?

"Want something to drink?" Nicola asked, opening the top box and handing me a triangle-shaped piece of dough. It was covered with a gooey white substance and speckled with different colors of green, red, and brown circular-shaped discs.

"It smells awesome. I'll just have some pop, er soda." I moved slightly and was pleased Josh kept his hand on my butt.

"The pizza should smell awesome. It was handmade by yours truly." Zac stood up and took a bow.

Nicola took a plastic container from the big shiny box. When she uncapped the top, it fizzed. She added small chunks of ice and then handed it to me.

I took a sip of the orange liquid and was in love. This was a different kind of soda than I'd borrowed from the Space Station. It was delicious. I put the glass down onto the counter and took a bite of the pizza.

It was everything Xron said it would be and more. The sensations hitting my tongue were jostling in a good way. I chewed the softness of the cheese and then got a hint of the crunchiest of the green and red things. What the heck? Something spicy was added into the mix. I couldn't wait for another bite. I took another, and another, and another.

"What's she still doing here?"

I gulped the piece down and turned on the swiveling chair to see who had entered the room. Great! Suzz had ventured into the building.

Josh shifted his hand from my bum pocket to the belt loop on my jeans, hooked his finger into it, and pulled me closer.

"I invited her," Nicola said somewhat defensively.

"For how long?" Suzz asked.

I have to admit I wasn't fond of her tone. My mouth full, I spurted out, "Just until I find my brother."

"Yeah, right. She'll be here forever."

I swallowed the last of my pizza before I was able to get a word in. "I promise."

"Suzz, chill out. She's not doing any harm." This was from Josh, who pulled his own stool even closer to mine, so we were almost joined together at the hip. It was a totally pleasant feeling.

"Well, let's hope it's soon," Suzz said. "Do you know how many calories are in a piece of pizza?"

"No, but I'm sure once again you're going to ruin all our fun and tell us," Zac said, grabbing an extra large piece.

Just as she was about to open her mouth, I looked over her shoulder toward the door that led outside and screamed. I jumped off the stool and almost *decapitated* Josh's arm.

"Bertie is that you?" I ran over to the six-foot mawl who had entered the room and hugged him. "I can't believe I found you."

"Excuse me," Suzz said, coming over and unwrapping my arms from around his torso. "His name is Albert, not Bertie, and he's my boyfriend." She stood in front of him, arms crossed. I hadn't seen someone so possessive since Zen borrowed Xron's tools without asking.

"Sorry, I guess I was mistaken." I slunk across the room and climbed back on the stool. I helped myself to another piece of pizza, taking comfort in the food and in Josh's arm, which snaked it's way naturally behind my body.

I was stunned into silence. Why didn't he recognize me? Why didn't he want anything to do with me? I chewed automatically, ignoring the conversation flowing. I needed help. I needed Rotsen.

"Excuse me, I'll be right back." I pushed Josh away, almost fell off the stool, and ran up the non-moving steps to my spare room.

"Rotsen, I need help," I begged, flopping down on the bed.

"You're right. I can smell pizza fumes on you, and you had better have brought me a piece or you'll be swimming with the fishes." He sat on the back of the *hanaglug*, leaves crossed. He was ticked off.

"Rotsen, I promise I'll bring you up a piece. But there are more important things to worry about. Bertie is downstairs," I said. "My brother, whom I needed to search the entire planet Earth for, is sitting in the kitchen, but he doesn't recognize me. He doesn't have a clue who I am.

"Bingo, bango, bongo. We've found your annoying brother, let's split this popsicle stand and, with the help of Ralb's maps, we'll be back to Zorca-twenty-three by tomorrow. But I'm so having a piece of pizza before we go." He did a little dance across the top of the *hanaglug*.

"I wouldn't be celebrating just yet. I think the humanoids, especially one named Suzz, have done a Vulcan mind meld on him. He doesn't know me." With a dramatic, diva flare, I dropped my head onto my folded arms.

"Umm, I don't know how to say this, but, April, wake up," Rotsen said, still fuming about the pizza I was sure. He obviously didn't have any patience for me.

"Rotsen, I'm not sleeping." I inhaled the sheets and sighed.

"Geeze, you need to watch more satellite. I meant it metaphorically. The last time Ralb saw you, you were an ananoid. OF COURSE, HE'S NOT GOING TO RECOGNIZE YOU IN HUMAN FORM. You only know it's him because of Zen's mind mapping. Ralb hasn't been answering his nosepiece. He doesn't know you're coming." He sighed. "Didn't he tell your BFF that you shouldn't come? Hello. Wake up and smell the caffeine."

"Oh, right. So how do I tell him?" I wanted to get back to Josh before there were three moons in the sky.

"Remember those pills Xron gave you, did you listen to what they were for, or did you just file them in your bag and forget about them? Wait. Don't bother answering, I already know. You need to slip one into his drink, and then he'll remember you." Rotsen folded his leaves in an extremely aggravating manner. "I think I deserve two pieces of pizza."

I kissed him on his top petal. "Rotsen, I'll bring you three pieces. Now where are those pills?"

He felt around in my *hanaglug* and wrapped his stem around the small vial, smirking at me as he got the lid off easily. "Just put one in the liquid he drinks, and we'll be headed home before nightfall."

Chapter Thirteen

I said a silent prayer to the Zorcan higher being that I had the right one. With the pill grasped in my hand, I bounded down the stairs straight into Suzz.

"FYI, stay away from my boyfriend." She jabbed her finger into my chest and put her face three inches from mine. "I know what you are, and I'll tell everyone if you even come within fifty yards of Albert. I'll expose you, witch."

"I have no idea what you're talking about," I said with a false sense of *brevity*. Or was the Earthling word *bravado*?

"I don't know where you came from, but it wasn't from around here. You are not of this world, and I'll expose you in a minute if you give me any grief." Her words were so filled with venom, she actually spit when she talked.

I was scared. How was I going to get my brother to remember me if I couldn't go within fifty yards of him? Even worse, I had no clue as to what a yard was.

I was in trouble.

Big time.

"There you are. I was wondering where you went. I missed you." Josh came and wrapped his arm around my waist. I was pleased he had lots of arm left. I guess I was skinny.

The people seemed to have multiplied as the house was now filled with teenagers. There wasn't any room to move, and I felt really hot.

He leaned forward and whispered in my ear. "Want to go for a walk? I'd like to be alone with you."

"Can I get my drink?" I noticed Bertie had gone into the kitchen. I grabbed my glass and then walked over to the fridge beside where my brother was standing. "Do I just push this lever to get the ice?"

"Yep! Here let me help." Josh held the lever for me, and I tipped my cup underneath. Suzz sauntered up to Bertie and pulled him away, but not before I did a move a Teenage Mutant Ninja Turtle would have been proud of. Well, maybe not one of them, but definitely a ninja move. I grabbed an ice cube in my hand from the magic lever on the door and then dropped it along with the pill into his frizzing liquid.

I held my breath as my brother took a drink. Either he'd recognize me in my Zorcan form, or he'd switch back to his original being in front of our eyes. Talk about a partee stopper.

Then Suzz glared at me, grabbed the drink out of his hand, and took a sip.

"Hey, April, I'd like you to meet my Owen." Nicola came up and joined our group, pulling a mawl with her. He wasn't nearly as handsome as Josh, but I could see how Nicola would think he was cute. His blonde curly hair fell over his left eye, so he appeared to be a bit of a Cyclops, but while he seemed to be missing an eye, his cute little face valleys more than made up for it. He had one on either side of his mouth and a dent in his chin. He reminded me of the guy from *High School Musical*, the one with all the wild curls.

"Josh, since you're closest to the fridge, can you fill me up?" Nicola asked, handing him her glass.

"Yes, madam." The clicking of the ice replaced the flow of the indoor waterspout.

"You drink a lot of water," I said, keeping an eye on Bertie, glad he'd gotten his drink back from Suzz.

"I drink between eight to ten glasses a day. It

helps me lose weight." Nicola took the glass back from Josh and gulped down half of it.

"You look fine to me," Owen said.

"Exactly the right thing to say. Let's go outside," Nicola said.

"April and I are going for a walk." Josh took my hand and led me outside, but not before I turned and looked at Bertie. He winked at me. Relieved, I grinned back.

My brother knew me. I glanced over at Suzz, and her face reddened. From the scowl on her face, it appeared she'd been sucking a sharp piece of quartz.

Oh, no, that couldn't be good. I allowed Josh to pull me outside and away from her evil glare.

My ears rang from the sudden silence of the outdoors. The pulsating sounds of *Green Day* were replaced with the muted guitars of *My Chemical Romance.*

"Do you live far from here?" I asked, feeling warm again, when he slipped his hand inside mine, crisscrossing our fingers.

"I'll show you." We walked to the end of Nicola's street and came to a dead end. We turned left along another street, and he pointed out a cute dwelling place.

"See that white house. That's where I live with my mom."

"You live in the White House?" I was impressed. I was meeting so many famous people today.

"Not the one in Washington." He laughed and then turned serious. "It's small compared to my friends' houses, but it's good for just the two of us." His breath tickled my ear and sent good shivers up my spine.

"Your house is big compared to mine." I snuggled close to him.

"April, you always say the right things to me." He squeezed my hand, and again I felt warm.

He turned and faced me, then slipped his hand from mine.

With the moon casting a glow around his hair, he resembled an angel with a small halo. He moved his hand under my freshly cut hair, and placed it on my neck like I was a piece of fragile rock dust.

"April, do you mind if I kiss you? You've been driving me wild all night," he said.

"Do what you must."

He smiled again and instinctively I tilted my head to the left as he moved his to the right. His lips landed on mine, and I panicked.

I couldn't breathe. It wasn't quite so bad as climbing all those steps, but my lungs couldn't receive any air. Frantic, I stepped back, away from Josh.

He released all contact with me, and I absorbed massive amounts of oxogyen.

Then I stepped forward. I wanted another kiss. Taking a deep breath to ensure I had enough air in my lungs this time, I wrapped both my arms around his neck and pulled him closer to me. I reached up and lowered his head to mine. Again I tilted my head one way, while he went the other.

Lips, soft and moist, zeroed in on mine. We pushed our lips against each other. Sadly, he broke contact, only to rejoin his lips to mine. He did this five times, and, yes, I know because I counted them.

"April, you're the best kisser ever," he said, when he drew away from me.

"I can honestly say, Josh, you're the best kisser I've ever had, too," I said, as his hands found their way back inside my jeans pocket.

"We'd better head back to the party. I don't want them to send out a search and rescue team for you." He led the way away from our spot. "I'll take you on a shortcut."

There was a bend in the road and a narrow dirt

path leading into some woods. He led me into the forest. Only the light of the moon allowed me to walk like a humanoid among the tree roots and not trip and stumble. I had the hang of my walking sticks, but to be on the safe side, I hung onto his hand. That was my excuse, and I was sticking to it.

"Have you lived here long?" I asked as we held hands. I wondered if we were going to do the kissing part again, but I didn't want to appear too anxious.

"I used to live in Campbellsville, but my dad got transferred to Bedrocktown two years ago, and so we had to move." Josh lifted me up and over a fallen log.

"What does your dad work at?"

There was a musical cricket concerto going on in these woods, and a croaking frog impatiently waiting for an answer.

"Umm, my dad died last year. He got cancer." I could tell by the light of the moon, he was still saddened by this.

"Was he in a casket?" I asked, prepared for his eyes to pee.

"Yes." He looked at me like I was strange. "But I don't want to talk about something sad. You make me happy."

"You make me hot." I answered. I guess it was the right thing to say because he squeezed my hand. He leaned toward me, and his soft lips zeroed in on mine. Then he sat back and didn't say a word.

I was afraid he might be mad at me for some reason, so I said the first thing to pop into my brain. "Do you know if you count the cricket's chirps in fifteen seconds and add that to thirty-seven, you'll have the outdoor temperature?"

"I found a girl who was cute and smart." Josh smiled down at me.

He and I were both lucky tonight.

We came to the edge of the woods and I gasped.

We were on a cliff overlooking a town. He let go

of my hand and sat down on a rock, which surprisingly felt like my own cave at home. He patted the smooth surface for me to join him.

So I did.

As soon as I sat down, he draped his arm around my shoulders and pulled me close.

"See all those lights over there." He used his other arm to point out a variety of different-sized buildings lit up like a baseball stadium.

I nodded, feeling very safe and warm cuddled in his arm. I wished I could stay here forever. No wonder Ralb didn't want to come back to Zorca-twenty-three.

"That's Suzz's family's farm. Her stepfather owns the town. The Gordons have more money than God. My dad worked for them before he died. Originally, they were a dairy farm and were the biggest milk producers in the state. Then her stepdad branched out and now has chickens, pigs, and horses."

"That's funny, because when I first met Nicola and Suzz, she was complaining because her mom wanted her to work during the summer." I switched my mind off my annoying brother and onto this mawl who was keeping me warm.

"Her mother came from a really poor family and thinks the kids should earn their own money. She and Suzz fight about it all the time."

"The river there is so pretty," I commented about the water sparkling by the light of the moon.

"It's a major tributary. It supplies all the town's drinking water. One day for something to do, I followed it, and it went for miles, ending in the lake on the other side of town." He grinned down at me. "I'll take you to the lake some night."

I opened my mouth to say I had already been there, but shut it. It would be more fun having Josh as my tour guide anyway. Besides, he might want to kiss me again, and I wasn't going to argue with that.

The lights from the farm as well as the lights from the downtown looked like a diamond necklace, glittering and shining in the moonlight.

I sighed.

"Was that a good sigh or a bad sigh?" He seemed unsure of my mood.

"Definitely good. I can't imagine a night more perfect than this." I removed his arm, but kept my hand inside of his and lay down on my back.

The night was clear with the full moon casting a haunting glow across the Earth, but I was more interested in the mawl by my side and the stars above. "See the bright star there, that's the Space Station and, if you count over three stars, there's a planet behind it called Zorca-twenty-three."

"I'm impressed, April, you sure know a lot about space. It's nice to see the stars and the constellations. We've had a lot of rain lately and couldn't see the stars at night." He lay on his side, looking at me.

"Josh, you need to look at the sky to see where these places are. See there's the Big Dipper." My stomach was doing gymnastics when I realized he was looking at me.

"I've never met a girl as fascinated with outer space as I am, but I'd rather watch your face. It just comes alive when you talk about stars." He leaned closer and brought his lips to mine again.

This time I knew what to expect. I felt oddly comforted that I could see my home planet while I kissed my Earth mawl.

I'd found my brother, my mission was complete, so now I could enjoy myself. I didn't even care anymore about Oscar. As far as I was concerned, I found my hunk of gold.

## Chapter Fourteen

"Josh, April, are you here? I need you back at the house right away," a voice called through the woods.

"Snap! Who the heck is looking for us?" Josh said angrily. I couldn't understand why he was upset. I was hot and needed some ice to cool down.

"It sounds like Suzz. Why would she want us?" I whispered.

"Probably to ruin my life," Josh muttered. "We're over here," he called. "What's up?"

"Figured you'd bring her here. Boy, you're not very original. Anyway, for some reason, Nicola is asking for you." Suzz pointed at me as she spit out the words.

"Bertie—sorry, Albert—what's the matter?" I glanced up at Suzz, then at my brother.

"I don't know, but she wants you."

"Me? Why does she want me?" I sat up. I wished they'd both go away so Josh would put his lips to mine again.

"She's in the bathroom throwing up. Zac didn't want to leave her, but she's calling for you." Suzz shrugged, flipped her hair over her shoulders, and folded her arms.

Bertie spoke again. "I told her you knew first aid."

"You know me? You remember me?" I said, jumping up and throwing myself into his arms. Which are nowhere near as nice as Josh's in any way, shape, or form.

"Of course, I do. You're my Oas." He rumpled my

147

hair. "My bratty sister."

"What are you talking about? Her name is April, not Oas," Suzz said, her tone indicated she was annoyed there was a conversation going on she didn't understand.

"No, she's Oas, all right. It stands for Older Annoying Sister," Bertie said, punching me in the arm. If I hadn't had witnesses, I would have thumped him so hard he would have ended up backwards in the black hole, but instead, I just smiled.

"My Albert is the brother you've been looking for?" Suzz sounded astonished.

"That he is. Now let's go and help Nicola," I said, as I reached around and grabbed Josh's hand and pulled him up so he was standing with the rest of us.

"Thanks for ruining the mood, you two," Josh said in a perturbed voice.

"You better not be getting into any mood or anything else with my sister." Albert/Bertie laughed.

"Of course not, we were just looking at the stars," I said pointing upwards. "Albert, you can see Zorca-twenty-three."

"Awesome," my brother said. "It's sure a long way away."

Without a backwards glance, he took Suzz's hand and dragged her through the woods.

"I wish Albert would show me the stars." Suzz pouted as she stumbled after him.

Chapter Fifteen

When I entered Nicola and Zac's house, it was empty and quiet. There wasn't any pulsating music or gyrating bodies, but it was a mess. Potato chip bags lay crumpled on the floor beside cans of every color and shape.

A floor lamp was overturned in the corner, and the cushions from the sofa were piled in the corner beside the stereo. I had no idea what happened there, but it didn't look like it had been fun.

I was so relieved Josh had taken me away from this party. I had a much better time with him alone. Maybe I could get Nicola fixed up fast, and then we could go back to looking at the stars and getting hot.

"Josh, can you bring me up a glass of water for her, and maybe Suzz can get a start on cleaning up the house?" I took command and bounded up the stairs, not waiting for an answer.

I checked the bathroom to find it empty and then went into her bedroom. I had only seen my spare room and Josh's room, so I was surprised at Nicola's. Where Josh's room was filled with boy stuff, Nicola's was pink. Everywhere there was the color pink. Pink walls, pink ceiling, pink furniture. Even all the coverings on the bed and floor were a light shade of the color. The accents and her nightgown were pink, too. Oh, stars! I felt like I was in a bad pink commercial.

On Nicola's windowsill was an array of plants with varying shades of pink flowers. Front and center in the middle of the pots was a Venus Fly Trap. I had to look twice. I thought it winked.

When I stared at it, it winked at me again.

My BFF from Zorca-twenty-three was here.

On Earth.

In Nicola's room.

I went over and removed the glass dome over top of Lehcarr, which created the terrarium like conditions she thrived in. I ran my fingers across her cilia, and she laughed. Stars above, I'd missed that sound.

"How did you get here?" I whispered to her.

"We'll talk later. You need to help the girl over there. She's been getting worse the entire time I've been here."

I put the dome back over her and went to Nicola's bed. She was easy to find in the room, because she was moaning and not pink. Far from it. She was a shade of green I'd never seen on a person before. Even the Edoricks weren't this pukey color.

I walked to her bed and felt her forehead. She wasn't hot, but then she hadn't spent any time with Josh.

"Hi, Nicola. I came as soon as I could. What's the matter?"

"April, thank goodness they found you. I went to the bathroom, and there was blood. It's not even close to when my period should be coming. I was bleeding. My stomach hurts." She groaned and then drew her sticks up to her chest area in a curled-up position.

"Here's the water, April." Josh put the glass on the table beside the bed. "Nicola, Zac called your mom, and she's coming right home. She should be here in about an hour."

"If I live that long." She moaned and rolled over on the bed, clutching her stomach.

"I'm going to go and help clean up, since the parents will be arriving shortly." Josh squeezed my arm as he went out the door.

Why was it every time he touched me I got hot?

"I'll be right back. There's something in my room I need to get for you," I said to Nicola. Without waiting for an answer, I ran from her room, down the hallway, and into my spare room. I was out of breath when I reached it and slammed the door.

"Finally, she shows up. Where's my pizza?" Rotsen sprawled across my pillow, his droopy leaves covering up his eyes. Great. Now I had to deal with a major drama king.

"Rotsen, I need your help." I panted. I figured if I ignored his attitude, it might disappear. No such luck.

"Always you needa my help, and I don't even get a stinkin' piece of pizza for my troubles. What is it now?" He sighed, putting his branches behind his petals.

"Nicola is sick, and I'm afraid she's going to need a casket." My eyes peed at the word.

"Okay, calm down. You always did get emotional. Girls, geeze. Okay, what's the problem?" He draped himself around until he'd morphed into a Dr. Phil position.

Just as I was about to tell him, a knock sounded at my door. I flung the comforter over Rotsen. "Come in."

Ralb poked his head in. After he shut the door, I uncovered Rotsen, who began hacking and coughing like he was oxogyen-deprived.

He paused, "You brought Rotsen? You travel to another planet in an entirely different solar system, and you bring your tootoo. You're such a girl. Well, at least you didn't bring Lehcarr."

"She's in Nicola's room," I whispered. "And I didn't bring her. I had no idea she was here until a while ago."

"She always was a determined Fly Trap," Rotsen said.

"Can we get back to Nicola? She's the one who needs our help." Turning towards Rotsen, I spoke. "Okay, her symptoms are bloody pee and stomachaches."

Rotsen turned white, which is quite an accomplishment for a tootoo whose color base is red, purple, and pink. I didn't want to think about that color right now. It reminded me of Nicola and that we needed to help her.

"What is it, Rotsen?" I crossed my fingers that it was going to be something fixable.

"Remember how you asked me to read up on the water chapter in the mist book? Remember the first time you told me you were going to bring me pizza and you never did? Not the second time when you said you were going to..."

"Okay, I get the point. Now tell us." I crossed my sticks on the bed and dropped my head into my hands.

"Fine. Page three hundred and fifty-five in the book says Bedrocktown uses well water. Her symptoms sound like a textbook case of Escherichia coli, or E. coli as the Earthlings more commonly refer to it. While a lot of E. coli doesn't affect any humans, the bad one is the E. coli 0157:H7."

"I saw a television show at Olivia's house about E. coli. What are the numbers and letters on the end? What on Earth is E. coli 0157:H7?" I asked, scared because it sounded so icky.

"If a town gets a lot of rain..." Rotsen started to say.

I interrupted him, "Josh told me he couldn't see the stars lately, because of all the rain they've been having."

Ralb nodded. "That's true. A really bad storm came through town, and I couldn't get any reception on my nose piece for days."

"That's why you didn't answer. Zen said it was

because you were in the clutches of a teenage girl," I said, smacking him on the arm.

"Well, I might have turned it off. Suzz is pretty hot," Ralb said dreamily.

"Please! She is so gross. Now Josh is the hot one."

"Anyway, before I was so rudely interrupted," Rotsen continued, "if there's a farm close to the well and a river with underground springs, there is a strong likelihood the fecal colliforms—"

"Would you speak English?" I was impatient to get to the source of Nicola's problem.

"Geeze, I thought you were educated. Okay, bacteria from animal poop can wash into the water supply. When humans drink the water, it gets into their systems and…"

"Where's my baby?" A shill voice boomed through the house. "Zac, where is Nicola?"

"Mom, she's in her room," a faraway Zac called out.

"I have to go help her." I jumped off the bed and ran towards the door. With my hand on the knob, I stopped. "How?"

"According to the mist book, if she just has the bloody diarrhea, she'll be fine. But the town's water needs to be fixed. The really young and old are especially susceptible."

"Nicola told me the neighbors on the street have died and been put in caskets," I told them.

"I know. They have the weirdest ceremonies for their dead." Ralb shook his head.

Ignoring him, I asked Rotsen, "How can I get them to listen to me? I have no proof."

"Here." Rotsen pushed a button on the mist book and out shot two pieces of paper describing the water problem.

Ralb shoved me off the bed. "They are a really nice family. Oas, you need to go and help her mom."

I ran from the room and straight into a strange woman who looked like Nicola twenty years in the future. She had hair the same color as her daughter and, well, me without the funky highlights. She had a figure, which appeared as if she spent a lot of time sampling food, but her clothes were tailored and fit her body perfectly.

"Do I know you?" she asked leaving the washroom and heading back to Nicola's room with a glass of water.

"I'm April, a friend of your daughter's. Don't give her that. It's what's making her sick." I knocked the glass out of her hand. We both stood there surprised as it shattered on the hardwood floor. The water flooded down the hallway.

"I'm always amazed at how much liquid is in a glass when it spills. Now who are you? And what in heaven's name are you talking about?" Nicola's mom said over her shoulder as she went and grabbed a towel and placed it on top of glass. "We'll clean it up later, along with the rest of the house. I'm not even going to worry right now about the two of them having a party. My daughter is more important."

I waved the papers under her nose. "Nicola is getting sick from the water in the town. She has E. coli poisoning, the E. coli strain 0157:H7. It's poisoning the town's water supply. Even little Olivia whom Nicola babysits is being poisoned. The well is beside Suzz's family farm."

A voice, filled with the familiar venom, hollered up the stairs. "You are such a liar."

Chapter Sixteen

I turned in time to see Suzz lunge toward me. She was going to tackle me, so I stepped aside. The momentum threw her off balance. She slipped on the wet floor and careened headfirst into the hall table. A blue vase on the top teetered with the sudden force. I tried to grasp it before it hit the floor.

I would have been successful if Suzz hadn't grabbed my ankle and pulled me down. The vase hit the floor just after I did.

"Mrs. Hargrove, you have no idea who you're dealing with. She's a bug, an insect with antennas and three eyes." Suzz pointed her index finger at me.

Oh, no, I was afraid of this. She drank some of Ralb's pop. When I put the pill in for him to identify me, she'd yanked it out of his hand. I held my breath. I didn't know what to do.

"Suzz, I will not have you acting like this in my house. I think you need to take a chill pill and relax. We're all a little excited right now. If you were Nicola's true friend, you would be more concerned about what is causing her to be sick, rather than picking on this poor girl. If you're going to be more of a hindrance than a help, I'd like you to leave now." Nicola's mom planted one hand firmly on her hip and pointed the other toward the exit.

"Sorry." Suzz tried to stand, but again slipped on the water.

I got up more easily. I guess being an ananoid in my former life gave me more flexibility. I held out my hand for her to take. She ignored it and succeeded in getting to her feet this time. Without a word, she turned and left us, stomping down the hallway, then down the stairs. She slammed the front door behind her.

"I never did like her, but she's Nicola's friend, so I've just kept quiet. I'm going to call our family doctor."

"I'll sit with Nicola and hold her hand while you're gone." I didn't wait for an answer and moved closer to Nicola's bed.

After a backward glance at her offspring, she ran to into the hallway. Soon I could hear her talking. In no time at all she returned to the room.

"April, is it? Thank you." Her mother hugged me and kissed me on the top of my hair.

"Thank you. I don't think my mom ever kissed me." I saw the strange look she gave me. "I have a lot of brothers and sisters, and she's busy with them."

"Sometimes Moms get occupied, but it doesn't mean they don't love you." She squeezed me extra hard. "I know with my job, I have to travel a lot, but I hope Nicola and Zac know in their hearts, I'm trying to make a better life for them."

"They know. In my case my brother is her favorite, but I just accept it." I shrugged to show there was no point in trying to change the unavoidable.

"Are you kidding me?"

I turned to see my brother standing behind us.

"Why do you think I left home? All I ever heard was 'Why can't you be more like your sister? Your sister got an Advanced marking on her mist book.' If anyone was favored, it was you."

I cringed, but the humanoids ignored the mist book comment.

"That's strange. All I ever remember hearing was 'Your older brother just got his Bronze Cross for stick carrying. Why can't you be more athletic like him?'"

Nicola's mother walked me over to Ralb and included him in our hug. "Sounds like your mom loves you both very much. I can't keep up with the electronics you kids have today. But don't tell Nicola about this mist book, or she'll be wanting one of those next. Remember your mom loves you."

"Yeah, I guess she does." I laughed.

I hugged my brother, something that seemed odd, yet comforting at the same time. She leaned over her daughter and put a mandible on her forehead, then bent and kissed the area.

"I'm going to head downstairs and make you your favorite." She left the room and rushed downstairs. No doubt to get back to her daughter's side as soon as she could.

Nicola already looked a little better. Maybe it was because we knew what the problem was. Or maybe because her mom was home. Whatever the reason, I was glad.

"How you feeling, Nicola?" I strolled over to her pink bed and looked down at her.

"I still feel a bit out of it, but better than I was." She patted the bed for me to sit beside her.

"Your mom is great." I reached out and held her hand, shifting a pink poodle to the other side of the bed.

"Sounds like yours is pretty good, too. I couldn't help overhearing you guys in the hallway. I'd like to meet her one day."

"I'd like that. I know she'd like you, too." I glanced over at Lehcarr swaying gracefully under the dome. How lucky was I to have my two BFF's in the same room?

"You have to go soon, don't you? Your mom will be worried about you," Nicola said.

"I think you might be right." I grabbed the bag that held my black hole clothes and brought it over to the bed. "I want to leave these for you. You'll have to put them in the machine because they probably need to be cleaned and ironed." I lifted them up to my nose. They didn't smell too bad, other than a bit sulphury from the asteroid. "I want you to keep them so you'll remember me forever."

"That is so sweet. Well, I'd like you to take something from me." She looked around her room. "Take Rachel!"

"Who's Rachel?" I asked.

"My Venus Fly Trap on the windowsill. She's a really good friend to me. That's why I named her Rachel from the show *Friends*." She waved her hand towards Lehcarr. "She's a good listener, and she's very pretty."

I was going to pee out my eyes, and I didn't even use the word casket. Her BFF was my BFF.

"April, don't cry. We'll see each other again. You promised to take me to the Black Hole shopping, and I'm going to hold you to that."

I leaned across the bed and hugged her tightly.

"Hello." A subtle knock interrupted us. Nicola's mom poked her head in the door. "Nicola, the doc is here to have a look see."

She opened the door wider and led in a man who commanded the room. He was as thin as a piece of spaghetti. His quick movements reminded me of Zen.

I was homesick. I had my BFF here, my brother here, a hunky mawl who liked to kiss me, but still I wanted to go home.

Fine, I'll admit it. I wanted my mom.

"Is this the young lady we have to thank?" He held out his hand and gave me a firm handshake.

"April, this is our town's doctor, Doctor Foster." Her mom sat on Nicola's bed in the space I'd just left.

"Well, young lady, I can't thank you enough for

copying all the information for us. The county well supervisors were coming next week, but your facts and figures certainly sped things up and probably saved five or six lives, not to mention the life of this young lady here in the bed." He patted Nicola confidently on the arm.

"Don't forget Princess Olivia."

"Olivia?" He looked at the older woman, confused.

"Olivia Ashbridge. Nicola babysits her."

"She's my patient, so I'll stop and take a peek at her on my way back to the office." He frowned. "That's the problem with E. coli. A lot of times it mimics the flu."

"Do you think that CastleRock farm is poisoning the town?" Nicola's mom asked.

"I think it's more likely to be Little Paulie's farm, because he's upriver from the well, whereas CastleRock is downstream," the doctor said, with the self-confidence every doctor on every planet I'd ever been on possessed.

"Do you really think that was the problem, causing the need for all the caskets?" I said, prepared for my eyes to pee, but they didn't. Hey, what was happening? I could say the word casket and no waterworks? Instead everyone in the room looked puzzled, as all eyes turned toward me.

Then the Doctor's authoritive voice broke the silence. "Without a doubt. Another town a few miles away had the same problem. That's why the county inspectors can't come until next week, but I know the course of treatment. We'll get working on Nicola right away."

I went over and hugged my friend as tightly as I could. "I'll miss you. You get better, and we'll keep in touch. Computers are amazing these days." Crap, my eyes were peeing like I'd drunk a gallon of that horrible water.

I took Lehcarr off the windowsill and kissed Nicola's mom on the cheek.

"I'm just going downstairs." I ran from the room and detoured towards my spare room.

"Hello, where's my pizza? I travel eons to get to this stupid planet, through numerous solar systems, and all I ask when I get here is for a stinking piece of pizza. And does she bring it to me? Nada! Lehcarr, when did you get here? I hope you're not waiting for pizza." Rotsen had twisted his leaves around into the shape of a gun. Thank stars, he didn't have another leaf to make bullets, or I'd be one dead humanoid.

"I'm magical, what can I say?" Lehcarr shrugged her leaves. "Oas, would you go and get him some pizza, because we don't need to hear him complaining all the way back to Zorca-twenty-three?"

"Right! Home!" Rotsen thrust his leaves in the air.

Lehcarr coughed, so we'd pay attention to her. "That's why I came. Zen sent me to tell you there's a major storm system heading this way. We have to use it to get back home. We need to leave in an hour at the latest."

"I can't leave this soon. I have too much to do. Besides Ralb has a map," I protested. "We can leave anytime we want."

"Apparently your brother has misplaced it. Don't ask me. I don't want to dwell on it anymore," Lehcarr said.

"I can't believe it. He is determined to ruin my life, no matter what planet I'm on," I fumed.

"Save it for someone who cares. Get me my pizza while I get you packed up here," Rotsen said. "By the way, where is the famous Ralb?"

"Downstairs, I think." I sprinted from my spare room and slid down the banister to reach the bottom more quickly than taking the stairs. Plus I'd always wanted to do it.

Breathless, I entered the kitchen to find Josh and Ralb there. Good, one thing down.

"May I have the last piece of pizza?" Without waiting for an answer, I snatched it along with a paper square and headed back upstairs.

Thrusting it at Rotsen, I snarled. "Here's your pizza. Now be quiet and eat. I have a lot to get done before we go. And make sure you don't get any mess on the covering, or I'll have your head on a silver platter."

"See, you do watch *The Sopranos*," Rotsen mumbled, his mouth full.

I didn't want to stay and watch him absorbing the mouth-watering treat. Why couldn't they have brought fresh, hot pizza up to the Space Station? I jogged downstairs and slammed to a halt at the kitchen door. I didn't want to look eager, even though my heart was beating so fast in my body I thought it was going to burst right out.

"What are you doing?" I asked my brother as he threw little clouds of whiteness into Josh's mouth. Or should I say tried to. More hit the floor than Josh's opening.

"We're having a contest." He told me as one ricocheted off the fridge. Doesn't it just show you how great my brother's aim is? I thought he was supposed to be an athlete.

"Umm, can I talk to your sister alone?" Josh asked Ralb

"Sure, fine. I'll go and see how Nicola's doing." My brother left without another word, very unusual for him.

"What's the matter?" I asked.

Josh had a look on his face like he'd lost his last friend. I didn't think it had anything to do with my brother leaving the room.

"I'm leaving tomorrow." He sat at the table and

picked up a piece of the white cloud, which was in a bowl in the middle of the table, and began pulling it apart.

"Where are you going?" I asked, glad he wasn't getting measured for a casket.

"France. My mom arranged a trip a long time ago. We're going to meet my cousins there."

"Why are you sad? It sounds awesome. I've always dreamed of going to France. Imagine visiting the Eiffel Tower and the Louve." I reached out and snagged his hand.

"Wow, those are the two places on my must see list." He looked down at my hand, which had somehow ended up between the two of his. "But you'll be gone when I get back. I might not see you again. I want you to have this."

He pulled a circular disc off his finger and gave it to me. It had a brown stone in the middle that changed colors when I held it up to the light.

"It's a tiger's eye stone. I'd like you to have it." He slid it on my finger.

"Josh, that is so sweet. Thank you." I leaned forward and kissed him on the cheek. My stomach felt all somersaulty, and my mouth felt dry. My throat felt like I had a rock lodged in it. I couldn't swallow. I think I was feeling love for this mawl. "We'll stay in touch. We can email even when you're in France. And no matter where you are, if you look at the third star from the Space Station, I'll look there, too, and it will be our secret code."

"April. I want to kiss you again." And he did. This time was different than the others. Now it felt, strange, almost wrong.

Oh, no!

"What is that white stuff in the bowl called?" I sputtered out.

"Popcorn. Why?" Josh said.

He tilted his head again. I ducked underneath

his arm.

"Oh, no!" I groaned. My head hurt. I moved my hand up to my hair and pretended to scratch my head. In reality, I was searching. Cripes, there it was. I checked the other side as well.

My antennas were starting to sprout.

"Ralb told me he was allergic to popcorn. I didn't realize you were too. I'm sorry April. I would never hurt you," Josh pleaded. "I love you. I know it's very soon to be saying it, but it's true, I do."

I collapsed against the stool in the kitchen, my energy sapped from my very being. "Call my brother, please!"

My stomach felt like I had just gotten off a roller coaster, while my arms and sticks were aching big time.

Josh ran from the room like a professional sprinter. I had to save myself. I didn't know how to handle ridding my body of the foreign substance.

"I don't know what happened. She was here just a minute ago." Josh glanced down toward me on the counter top. "Aww, look at the cute bug. I guess it came in through the open door." He used a straw to lift me up, then set me down on the tiles. "Now she's gone. The back door is open. Maybe she went out there," Josh said as he and my brother came into the kitchen. He ran outside, leaving Ralb alone with me.

"Psst! Ralb, I'm down here. It's me. Over by the popcorn bowl." I darted up the legs and across the table to get his attention. When he finally noticed me, I screamed, "Quick, pick me up. We have to go. Lehcarr said she was sent here to get us back home. I can't let Josh know who I really am." My triads quivered in panic.

"I can't find your sister anywhere." Josh came inside and quietly closed the door. He sank down in the wooden chair. It was all I could do not to leap onto his lap. But knowing my present state of morphing, he'd likely kill me. I mean what Earthling wants a three-eyed ananoid jumping on him, even if he did profess undying love for her only a short period of time before.

"Don't worry. She'll be fine. She tends to overreact about things. You know how girls are. Ouch!"

My brother will end up with a nice sized bruise from my pinchers for that comment.

"April is different. I wish I weren't going away tomorrow. I would have liked to spend more time with her." Josh flipped open the pizza box. He seemed surprised it was empty.

My brother did have a soft side. I appreciated it when he went over to Josh and laid a soothing hand on his shoulder. "I'm sure you'll see her again."

"You really think so? I'd really like to get to know her better." Josh ran his hand through his hair.

"Oh, you'll see her again, I'm sure," my brother insisted. "If not, there's always Suzz."

Ralb was going to pay big time for that one.

"Anyway, I have to run upstairs and grab a couple of things, then I'm heading home. Nice meeting you, Josh. Send a postcard."

I poked my head out of Ralb's shirt pocket for a last look at Josh. I didn't know ananoids/humanoids could cry, but I did.

## Chapter Seventeen

Ralb pulled the door of Nicola's house shut and walked down the street. He stopped once he got to the end, where the streetlights stopped and the road was bathed in semi-darkness. The only light came from the distant full moon.

"Okay, what's the next step?" He unlocked my *hanaglug* and spread it open, allowing Lehcarr and Rotsen freedom to breathe.

"Zen told me we had to find a place called CastleRock." Lehcarr took deep breaths now that she was out of her dome. She reached up, grabbed, and snapped a mosquito as it was about to land on Ralb's arm. "Yumm. That pizza did not fill me up."

"It was a measly little piece, and I had to share it." Rotsen agreed. "Never again am I traveling all the way to Earth only to find myself sharing a piece of pizza. Do you know how long I dreamed of the melted cheese, the morsels of pepperoni?"

"No, we don't know and, no, we don't care. I think we have more important things to think about than you and your stupid pizza cravings," Lehcarr said, voicing our thoughts.

"There's no CastleRock around here. The town is called Bedrocktown. Lehcarr, I think you've gotten us lost." Ralb looked around for a sign.

"Says the guy who misplaced our butterfly map to get home," I said, upset at our sudden departure.

"I can't be expected to remember everything. I was looking at the map when Suzz walked by. I got distracted." He shrugged. "I kissed her."

"What?" Great. Here, I thought I was the only

one of us who got to experience "the kiss," and my brother has to steal my thunder, so to speak.

"How was it?" I asked, morbidly fascinated to see if the feelings I'd encountered with Josh were near to what he'd had with Suzz.

"It was gross." He shrugged. "I don't know why humanoids think it's fun to place their lips on one another. It was all I could do to not vomit."

I tried to keep my face hidden inside his pocket, so he couldn't see how his news affected me. So Josh's kiss made me hot, and Suzz's kiss made my brother almost lose his dinner.

Mind you, anytime she came near me, I wanted to do that as well, so maybe it was just her.

Then I remembered why the name CastleRock was so familiar.

Ignoring my brother, I said to Rotsen, "CastleRock is the name of Suzz's family farm."

"Okay, let's hurry. We have to climb to the highest point and wait until the storm hits, then we'll slingshot home," Rotsen said, like it was an everyday occurrence.

"That doesn't sound right. You mean there are no math calculations involved, nothing I need to figure out?" I asked.

"Nope! Zen did the math. Said all we had to do was wait for the second lightening bolt and *voilà*. I guess he knew better than to rely on you and your math calculations to get us home." Rotsen stuck out his tongue.

I was so glad I'd neglected to bring him more pizza.

Ralb gathered the *hanaglug* together, and once again we set off. "It doesn't look like it's going to rain."

"Zen is never wrong." Ralb picked up the pace.

"That's true," I agreed, clinging to my brother with my antennas. He was in a lot better shape than

I was. I wondered though how he would have managed all the steps in Olivia's house. He never even broke a sweat. But I had never seen Ralb more nervous or scared. It was a big responsibility getting us all back to Zorca-twenty-three in one piece. I was drenched just holding on, and it hadn't even started to rain yet.

I spoke too soon.

The clouds opened up, and a downpour began. We were soaked through, well, I should say Ralb was soaked through, because we were tucked inside. We, of course, weren't.

Ralb stopped at the iron gates intertwined with a massive C and R, signifying I assumed CastleRock. Her farm looked even more impressive close up than it did when I had viewed it with Josh. I lost count at ten barns. They looked bigger than any houses I'd ever seen with their red brick veneers and black wooden shutters.

The house was three times the size of the largest barn. There must be a heck of a lot of spare rooms in it, probably enough for my entire family. The house was constructed in the same brick as the barns, but three stories high. A porch ran along the front of it and five different groupings of chairs and loungers were arranged on it.

We looked up. The highest point was the top of a feed silo. Stars, it was high. "Okay, people are we ready for this?" I screamed from inside my brother's pocket.

"What are you doing here? Haven't you caused enough damage to me and my family?" Suzz came around the side of the silo.

"Oh, no." Ralb stopped in his tracks.

He was even more intense than before. He pretended he didn't hear her as he put one hand on the metal ladder.

"Albert, I thought you liked me, but your sister

has been smearing my name all over town," Suzz said.

I didn't need to see her face to know she was standing with one leg in front of the other one, major hostility written in her entire attitude.

"I so did not," I said.

Of course, she couldn't hear me in my ananoid state, but Ralb could.

"I don't think she did," Ralb said. How cool is that? My brother defending me to a psycho girl. I was impressed.

"Tell her it wasn't her family's farm. They are upriver from the current flow. It was the farm owned by Little Paulie of the Licketty Fingers Ice Cream Parlor," I said. I also wanted to add she needed to take kissing lessons if there was such a thing, but then I figured this was neither the time nor the place to brag.

He repeated what I said. I was relieved to see her nod.

"Makes total sense," Suzz said, the touch of snobbiness gone from her tone.

"Tell her to go and see Nicola." I nudged my brother. "The doctor was the one who told me about the currents, so they know it wasn't her fault."

I leaned further out of his pocket than I should have in order to watch her leave. Almost falling out, I righted myself and looked up to see something glittering at her neck.

"Ralb, she's wearing the butterfly necklace. She's wearing our map." I jabbed him with my antenna.

"Can I have a kiss goodbye?" He asked as he walked closer and wrapped his arms around her waist. Okay, from what I can see about boys on your planet Earth, they are major fickle. One minute he's telling Lehcarr, Rotsen, and me about how yucky her kisses were and then the next, he's begging for another one.

I have to say I'm glad my Josh was never like that. I knew where I stood with him. I didn't want to go there, thinking about my guy, or I'd end up peeing out my eyes.

Watching them from inside his shirt pocket, I had the similar experience as when I went flying through the Black Hole. I almost vomited. Right in the middle of this embrace, but I put my wanting to puke aside and did what had to be done.

A lightening bolt tore across the sky, followed by a crack of thunder. The rain pummeled us. I ducked back inside his shirt pocket and waited for the opportune time to pounce.

Using my antenna and stealth-like moves, I unclasped the necklace and scurried around to her shoulder. I dropped it into his waiting hand.

She broke off the kiss. "Yuck, I think a bug just flew down my shirt."

She swatted herself. It was all I could do not to giggle, since by that time I was already safe in my brother's pocket.

"Tell her Nicola wants to see her," I whispered.

Ralb muttered, "Let me handle this."

"I know it flew in my blouse. Did you see it? It was the ugliest creature I've ever seen.

Before I could swat her myself, Ralb patted his pocket to calm me down, then turned toward her. "Suzz, I really enjoyed our time together, but you're too good for me. You deserve better."

"You're absolutely right. Besides, it never would have worked out. My family never would have approved of your sister."

She gave up looking for the insect, but I was ready to smack her one. Luckily, before I was arrested for homicide on your planet, my brother realized my intentions and saved me or rather Suzz.

Ralb grabbed his shirt pocket and held me

inside, knowing after that last comment, I'd tear her apart limb by limb.

"Maybe in another life. Bye, Albert! You never were a Bertie to me!" Suzz kissed him quickly on the cheek and ran up her driveway.

"Okay, folks, are we ready now?" Ralb jumped up and hooked his arm over the first bar and pulled himself up as if he were doing chin-ups. In no time at all, he had scampered up the side of the silo and, with everyone else tucked into my *hanaglug*, we were on top.

Good thing we had left the climbing to him because, frankly, I was totally drained. I was torn up inside. I wanted to go home and see Mom, but on the other hand, or rather antenna, I had all my friends both from home and here.

On the bright side though, I could always come back on the next passing asteroid. With those thoughts in mind, I closed my eyes and prayed to the stars above that we'd make it back to Zorca-twenty-three in one piece.

"Now we just have to wait for the right minute," I said, wrapping the tiger's eye tighter around my antenna. "If you so much as breathe a word of Josh to Progri, I'm so going to..." I couldn't finish my sentence.

It happened.

The second jolt of lightening hit the top of the silo and, before I realized what had happened, we were airborne. My stomach had just settled from changing back into its normal state. Now it tumbled as if there were a hundred dragonflies twirling and twisting inside, in more turmoil than when Josh kissed me.

I tucked myself further into Ralb's pocket as we hurtled through space, passing a satellite, spiraling out of control. I caught the signals being beamed down to Earth and reminded myself I'd have to tune in to a really cool show called *The O.C.* Anything with sand and cute boys was okay with me.

I had a moment of remorse as I wondered what my Earth friends were doing. I wouldn't be able to discuss the latest clothing styles with Nicola or spend more time with Josh.

Right, I was going back. As soon as I got back home, kissed my P.B. and maybe talked her into traveling with me, I'd be back to planet Earth.

I had an interplanetary passport to fill up.

I thought of Josh, Nicola, and even Suzz and crossed my antennas they wouldn't forget me.

I wouldn't forget them, even Suzz. Hey, maybe I could make a deal with Lehcarr to eat her. She'd gotten rid of Kaj for me. (Unfortunately, Kaj had resurfaced, which reminded me I was going to have to have a chat with Lehcarr about that.) But knowing Suzz, she'd cause my BFF indigestion.

Epilogue

I awoke, rubbed my eyes, and looked around surprised at how green and lush everything was. Birds chirped in a leafy tree and, as I lay on a cobblestone street, I inhaled the smells of baking bread.

This was definitely not the Zorca-twenty-three I remembered.

Ralb was lying under a nearby oak tree. Several acorns fell and clunked him on the head, waking him up.

"Oas, you're a person again," my brother said, glancing at me.

I didn't believe him. I sat up and took an inventory. Yep, I had arms, sticks, hands, and when I felt my head, I still had the Damon haircut.

"What the heck do you think happened?" I asked Rotsen, who was lying beside me, soaking up the warm sun, his leaves and petals reaching toward the golden orb.

"It appears, *mes amis*, we're lost," he said, donning for some unexplainable reason a French accent.

"I know we're lost. What I'm asking is what happened to me? How come I'm not an insect any longer?" I asked as I smelled those lingering aromas of bread, mixed with the sweeter smell of pastries.

"My guess is, *ma petite*, that because you were an ananoid when you traveled through whatever black hole Ralb led us, it reversed the process. Therefore you turned back into a humanoid." Rotsen had adopted a smug and condescending attitude.

"Okay, then Mr. I-Know-Everything, why didn't Ralb change back? He went through the black hole as a humanoid, so why is he still a human?" I stood up with my hands on my hips. I'd learned a thing or two about attitude from Suzz.

"Maybe because I'm a mawl, and we're tougher about these things." He laughed and ruffled my hair.

"Ralb, I don't think we went through the black hole. I wonder what planet we're on? Look at the funny helmets all those people are wearing. I thought Earth was the only planet populated by humans."

We had a roadside seat as we watched more than one hundred men wearing helmets and tight shirts and shorts riding two-wheeled dragonflies.

It appeared to be a race of some sort as they kept their heads down and pedaled fast. One man stood beside us and tossed cups of water at them. I thought he was rude, but the bikers seemed to like it, so I guess it was okay.

"Does anyone have any idea what this is all about?" I whispered behind my hand so as to not distract anyone.

"If I had to guess, I'd say it was the Tour de France," Rotsen answered.

I was glad he knew, but I have to tell you, I wish just once I could ask him a question and have him shrug his puny little petals and say, "I don't know."

"Okay, so what's that?" I asked, since he didn't give us any details.

"It's a bicycle race around France. They go a certain number of miles or kilometers every day and whoever is in the lead gets a new shirt." Rotsen clung to the butterfly necklace as the riders whizzed by.

I sat down on the cobblestones to watch the race. Fans were waving red, white, and blue flags. I thanked my lucky stars I wasn't supposed to suit up.

Jane Greenhill

For one thing I wasn't athletic enough, though I'm sure Ralb could have held his own. My second reason is I didn't think I'd be able to squeeze into those tight outfits. It was bad enough trying to get into my jeans.

When it appeared the last racer had left the village, I turned my attention to the people entering the small shops that lined the old stone street.

Despite the smell of bicycle tires and sweat, the bakery smells overpowered my senses. I couldn't help myself. I got up and walked over to the window, eyeing the pastries on display. There were rows upon rows of chocolate donuts, chocolate éclairs, and chocolate swans made of pastry.

I was in chocolate heaven. I was about to enter La Patisserie when I thought I should ask the obvious.

"Zen didn't say anything about chocolate, did he?" I called over to my brother.

"Not that I remember." Ralb yawned.

How could he be tired when there were all these goodies to sample? "Instead of sleeping, how about you look at the map and try to figure out where we are and how we can get back home?"

I turned back around to head into the shop and ran smack into him. I almost pinched his cheek to make sure I wasn't dreaming. But I wasn't. My favorite star who was nominated for the golden statue, Oscar, stood a mere six millimeters away from me.

"What are you doing here?" I asked, shocked.

He gave me a slow grin. A smile accented by cheekbones I had watched on satellite TV over and over and over again.

"Darling, I'm just visiting." He looked down at me. "I'm doing the opening for a new movie exhibit, and I just thought I'd take a break."

"Of course," I stammered.

I Was a Teenage Alien

"I have a bit of time, would you like to join me for a café in the café?"

About to nod, I glanced behind him and squealed. Without a goodbye I shortened the distance between us and jumped into Josh's arms, wrapping my mandibles and walking sticks around him.

"I thought I'd never see you again," I said as I feathered my mandible through his soft brown curls.

"It must be fate. My mom wanted to come to this town. There's a famous celebrity who lives near here, and she was hoping to see him." He laughed as he placed me back onto the ground. I was happy he kept one mandible around me.

"You must be April." A femawl extended her hand in my direction. "I've heard a lot about you."

"Mom, don't give away all my secrets," Josh said, as he squeezed me like humanoids squish toilet paper on television.

I stepped closer to his P.B. and whispered in her ear. "He's right over there." I nodded toward the cafe. "He asked me to join him for coffee, but I'd rather spend time with Josh. So take my place." I gave her a gentle push in the direction.

"You must think a lot of my son to blow off an Oscar-nominated celebrity." She squeezed my arm and then headed to the table where he sat.

"Wow. I couldn't help but overhear. Thanks." With a quick glance toward his mom, Josh leaned down and kissed me.

His lips tasted like strawberries, a whole heck of a lot nicer than the shampoo.

I rested my mandible on his shoulder. I moved the ring he gave me so it caught the sunlight and reflected small jets of sparkles.

"Gross," Ralb said, making gagging noises. "What do you think our P.B.s would say?"

"Luckily, they're not here." Now go away. I

175

mouthed the words to him, but like the typical annoying brother he was, he ignored me.

"Maybe if you can stop swapping spit with Josh. No offense, man." He looked at my mawlfriend. "You would see they're right behind you."

"Yeah, right." I didn't believe him, but so that he'd leave us alone, I glanced behind me.

Stars above, my P.B.s were no more than a meter away. I screamed for the second time that morning. Tearing myself away from Josh, I sprinted toward them and fell into their mandibles. At this rate, I'd be able to handle Olivia's steps no problem.

I was fit.

"No way." They tapped me three times on both sides of my head, and I grinned at the familiar Zorcan love hug. "How did you get here?" I asked, holding my Zorca-twenty-three P.B. at mandibles' length.

"It's been forever since we interplanetary traveled. You kids aren't the only ones allowed to have fun." She smiled as she flicked a loose strand of bright red hair behind her ear. I peered at her clothing and was relieved to find she was wearing normal clothes, almost identical to what Josh's mom wore, blue jeans and a red sweatshirt. Mom clothes.

"You've been here before? You never told me."

"Oas, I did have a life before I had offspring." She laughed.

My mawl P.B. had been silent until this point. Now he grinned. "We actually met on this planet, and we would have stayed, but there's no place like Zorca-twenty-three." He wrapped his mandible about my mom.

"Then why didn't you come for Ralb?" I asked as my head ping-ponged from one to the other.

"I couldn't get the time off work. I'd promised your mom a trip for our wedding anniversary, so I needed to raise the funds." He leaned over and whispered in my hair. "Besides, I wanted you to realize how special Zorca-twenty-three is."

Well, that didn't work. Earth had my mawlfriend, something sadly missing on my home planet.

Then Josh's familiar scent of strawberries and fresh clean soap enveloped me.

"I'm Josh." He held out one hand to my P.B. or my dad—or I'm not sure what he was—while with the other he took my mandible.

His hand, or mandible, or whatever, was ignored. My P.B.s gave him the same love hug they had given me. Josh was speechless, but smiled.

"He's a keeper," my mom whispered.

"Son, I'm very hungry. How about we head inside and have some of those fancy desserts?" my dad said as he wrapped an arm around Josh's shoulders.

"Can I get you anything?" Josh asked

"Whatever you think I'd like," I said, not really concentrating on what I was saying. When they were safely inside the store and Ralb was busy chatting up one of the waitresses, I turned to my P.B. "I'm going to miss him so much." My eyes started to pee. "There's no one like him in any solar system."

She nodded. "So tell him the truth. If he's the mawl I think he is, he'll love you no matter what you tell him."

"He'll think I'm nuts."

"If he really loves you, he'll understand. If not, it wasn't meant to be, and you're meant to return to our planet alone to procreate with Gorget." She leaned forward to smell a rose that decorated the middle of a round table.

I shivered at the thought of spending eternity with the two-timing Zorcan. "How about I stay here?"

"You can only remain on Earth for a maximum

of six months, then you must return, or your body will change back to its original shape."

"My life sucks, big time." My stomach ricocheted. How did my freaking life get so screwed up?

"Oas, I know how you feel."

"How can you know how I feel? You've never had to make a difficult decision."

She didn't bother to answer me, but instead gave me *the look.*

"You look pale and upset. Have you taken any of the pills since you landed?" she asked, concerned.

"No, I didn't need to," I said, somewhat bragging.

"Take one. That's what they're there for, and it will help you." She paused. "Just make sure you don't take the round ones."

I was too wound up to ask her why. I found my *hanaglug* and popped one, swallowing it dry without a drink to wash it down.

Immediately, a calmness swept through me. It wasn't a difficult decision to make. Either spend six months here and end up a bug or head back to Zorca-twenty-three and end up a bug.

"I could handle being a bug again." It sure beat being married to Gorget.

"It's your choice."

"What's your choice?" Josh set three chocolate treats in front of me. I sank down into the chair at the table. How could I not love this mawl? He brought me numerous desserts. Gorget wouldn't have even brought one.

Before I could change my mind, I grabbed his hand and pulled him away from the group. "Ralb, touch those and you're dead meat."

"What's the matter?" Josh asked as I led him behind a tree, the trunk wide enough to hide us from prying eyes. He wrapped his arms around my torso

I Was a Teenage Alien

and pulled me close. "I want to kiss you again."

"I want to as well, but I have to tell you something first." I fingered the material of his white T-shirt.

"You're breaking up with me?" His mouth was set in a terrible down-shape.

"No, of course not. Here's the thing. I'm an alien." I bravely raised my eyes up to look at his, and he was smiling. "Remember at Nicola's when you couldn't find me, and you picked up that bug with a straw. It was me."

"What was you?" The hairy parts over his eyes raised and almost joined together.

"I was the bug." I slid out of his arms and bent down to pick up a leaf, which an ant scurried off.

"Get out of here."

"Okay, I kind of thought you'd feel that way." I pulled the leaf apart. "It was nice knowing you."

"Hang on a second." He pulled me back. "You're serious. You're a bug." He lifted up my hair and searched for some proof. "But you're mom and dad are normal. They're not"—he paused—"ananoids."

"Yeah, they are."

"Oh, I get it. You're adopted."

"No, Josh. My parents transformed when they came to this planet." I shrugged. "Anyway, that's why I didn't want to tell you. I knew you'd hate me."

"April, I don't hate you. I'm trying to understand. I mean, when your girlfriend tells you she's an alien, it's not something you can prepare yourself for."

"True," I admitted. "I've never seen it on Dr. Phil."

He sank down onto the grass and dropped his head into his mandibles. He glanced up at me, then down at the grass again. "I think it's a pretty lame way to break up with me."

"I have proof." I ran toward my *hangalung* and

179

grabbed the pill vial along with a glass of water that I ripped out of Ralb's hand.

I jogged back toward Josh and handed him the pills. "If you take one of these, you'll see me in my original form."

He glanced up at me and without a word, popped open the vial, and poured a couple into his hand. He ate them dry without the water. I guess after Bedrocktown, he was a little water shy.

I waited and watched as his face twisted from shock to amusement. I started to walk away, but he jumped up faster than I'd ever be able to manage.

"I don't care what your name is or where you came from. I'll follow you to the ends of the solar system, my little E.T." He kissed me, and then bit his lip. He glanced over my shoulder, and I turned to see what had caught his attention. He stared at his mom, laughing with the movie star. "April, I'm sorry. I would follow you to your planet, but I can't leave my mom here on Earth all by herself."

"I understand." I wasn't being completely honest, but I'd watched enough soap stories on satellite to know that's what I had to say. Whether I meant it or not.

I strolled back to the table and flopped down onto the wrought iron chair. The chocolate on the table mocked me. I didn't want it, couldn't eat it. I had a lump in my throat the size of a hunk of charcoal. Those darn pills did nothing for me. My eyes peed. I wiped them with the back of my mandible. Rotsen was on the middle of my table, snuggling up to the rose. I wasn't about to tell him the flower had thorns. With his attitude, I'd let him find that out for himself.

My mawl P.B. joined me and wrapped a mandible across my shoulders. He didn't say anything. He seemed to know I didn't want to hear any words of wisdom. Besides words can't fix a broken heart.

"So when do you leave?" Josh asked as he stood by our table.

I hid my face, not wanting him to know the effect he had on me. "Soon."

Josh pushed back his chair and stood up. "I need to go and think."

"I'll come with you," I said, not wanting to waste a minute without him.

We strolled down the bumpy, uneven, stone steps, and even the sight of my celebrity didn't distract me.

"I wish I could stay," I whispered.

"I know, sweetheart. I wish we could be together forever." He took my mandible and squeezed it. "I have such plans for the future, and I want you to be a part of them."

"Like what?" I sat on a low brick wall, the stones cold on my butkus.

"Well, I was going to go to college and go into the science field. Then my dream is to be an astronaut."

"That's it." I punched him in the arm. "I can stay here for six months. Then you can become an astronaut and visit me."

His eyes widened and a slow smile crossed his lips. He gave me a look, a glance that warmed my insides to a rapid boiling point. "I'll be busy studying, and the time will fly by."

"Just stay away from Suzz."

"April, you're the one I love, my favorite little alien."

And then he kissed me.

And believe you me, his kisses were out of this world.

\*\*\*\*

My Earth mission was complete.

I glanced over at Ralb. He was holding a cup of water for the riders. Good. I was glad he was distracted. All I needed was for him to ruin a moment. Finally, Josh and I were alone.

I had just turned my back on my brother when he tapped me on my shoulder.

Ice cold, salty water soaked my face and dripped onto my shirt. My sibling had accomplished what annoying brothers did no matter what planet they were on.

He'd ruined my moment.

"What? " He raised his shoulders in a shrug. "I was just trying to help Josh see what you really look like. "

I rubbed my eyes to rid them of the stinging liquid. My eyeballs burned. Ralb tossed an empty salt shaker to the ground and took off running.

As soon as I could see, I was going to kill him. Nice and slow I'd torture him, enjoying every single minute.

Two-wheeled dragonflies whizzed by. But Josh was no longer around.

Stars above.

I was lying on my back in the middle of a plush red carpet, my mandible attached to another dried up stick.

Glitters and sequins swished across my face as celebrities didn't even stop to help me up.

That's when reality hit me.

Smack dab in the mandible.

I was back in my original form. When I glanced to the left, Josh was beside me, the cutest praying mantis I'd ever have the pleasure to kiss.

Stars above, when Josh took the pill to see me in true form, he must have also taken one of the ones to change him into an ananoid.

I really wasn't in any hurry to get back to Zorca-twenty-three.

Life was pretty good on Earth.

Which was just as well.

As I had no idea how I was going to get home.
The end—for now...

## About Jane Greenhill

Born with a passion to read and write and heavily influenced by Nancy Drew mysteries, Jane Greenhill recalls her first writing experience on an old Underwood typewriter, plunking away at the keys while she wrote about hiding clues in oak trees. Fast forward through marriage and motherhood, and Jane's now advanced to a laptop and her characters speak to her from other planets.

**Other Titles by Jane Greenhhill**

*Vortex to the Ojibwa*

*Booty Call for Murder*

LaVergne, TN USA
13 April 2010
179137LV00004B/2/P